CAMPERVANS Cooking AND CORPSES

TYLER RHODES

Copyright © 2023 Tyler Rhodes

Dedicated to everyone who's ever thought, *"Blow this for a game of soldiers,"* and gone off to do something different.

It's never too late...

Chapter 1

"Max!" Minnie, although you called her anything but Min at your peril, smiled, then frowned, my ex-wife's dimples making my stomach flutter same as always.

"Hi. Just thought I'd come and say goodbye like I promised."

"I'm glad you did. I'm always pleased to see you. You know that."

Anxious, my best friend and energetic Jack Russell Terrier, whined from beside me.

"Yes, you too, Anxious," laughed Min, bending to ruffle his head.

My devoted dog wagged excitedly and sat, knowing the deal.

Min reached behind her to the small console table hidden by the front door then asked, "Now, what do I have here? Who could this be for?"

Anxious barked, more than happy to play along with the game.

"For you? You wouldn't want this, would you?"

Anxious held up a paw, drool hanging to the step.

Min giggled, her long dusty hair sparkling in the early morning light, then gave him his treat.

Gentle as always, he took it then moved over to the generous front lawn and settled down to enjoy his final treat before we hit the road.

"You're really doing this?"

"I sure am. We're heading off right now. I just wanted to say goodbye. And it's not too late to come along," I chuckled, but meaning it. Nothing would make me and Anxious happier than for the love of our lives to join us on our epic road trip.

"Don't be silly. I have work. And we aren't even married anymore."

"No, but we're friends."

"So you genuinely did it? All you said you would?"

"I did. I know everything was my fault, and I was a nightmare to live with. That's the life of a 3-star Michelin restaurant chef. Never home, always grumpy, continually stressed. I was burned out and took you down with me. It took us breaking up for me to realise what an idiot I'd been, but yeah, I quit. I'm done with that life for good."

"I wasn't sure if you were telling the truth."

"When have I ever lied to you? How could I?"

"True," admitted Min.

"That rubbish little house is sold, and you know I've been living with Mum and Dad for a while until I sorted everything out, but I got rid of the last of the furniture and now it's the open road."

"Are you sticking to your plan about cooking?" asked Min, still not quite believing I was genuinely doing this.

"Oh yes. I'm beyond sick of posh food. If I never see a foam or a reduction again in my entire life, it will still be too soon. It's back to basics for me and I absolutely cannot wait. One-pot cooking every night. I can't bear to think of faffing around making fancy meals a moment longer. It's freedom. A new start. A new me. No more grumpy chef. Now I'm able to do whatever I want."

"Including growing your hair. You look so different. And the beard. You've got grey streaks in with the brown."

"Tell me something I don't know! It's been short for so many years that I never realised. But I guess brown with a smattering of grey makes me look distinguished, right?" I studied Min's blue eyes, the pupils enlarging as she laughed. She deserved so much better than what I'd given her and now she had it. How could I ever have been so dumb as to put my career before our relationship? Shows you don't automatically grow wise just because you get older and get a good job. If anything, you become more stupid, thinking money and status equals a happy home life when in fact it's all too easy for it to create the opposite.

"You look relaxed is what you look. About time too. And your eyes are calm, not manic. They even seem lighter, almost green instead of blue."

"That's what I thought! Can your eyes change colour?"

"No, I don't think so, but who knows? You definitely seem very different though."

"I feel different. Min, I just wanted to say, I'm sorry. I know I've said it a million times before, but I truly am. For everything. The pain I caused, the suffering, the hurt and upset. The lonely nights. All of it."

"Max, it's water under the bridge."

"Not for me, it isn't. You know I still love you, but I understand you've moved on. Is there someone here?" I asked, peering around her slim figure clad in simple jeans and a green vest to check the hallway for signs of coats or shoes. A hallway that used to be ours, along with the house. I'd signed it over to her gladly after the divorce. It was the least I could do.

"No, of course not. It's only been a year. Most of that has been spent hunting for a different job, getting settled in once I found one, and finally sorting out our junk. You packing it all in was a wake-up call for me too."

"So you have enough money?"

"Yes. You were very generous. I'm glad we just split everything, and there were no arguments over the finances."

"I told you, you could have had it all. You deserved it."

"Half was enough. And besides, the investment house sold for a fortune and we both earned great money. But now you've sold your new house too?"

"I hated that place. It's what I need. A clean break. Time to finally travel. I was straight into the kitchens after school and I feel like I haven't seen daylight for fifteen years. This is going to be so great."

"It's been a busy and strange year for us both. Max, I'm sorry too. I wish I hadn't divorced you. We could have just gone our separate ways, but I got so angry that final day when you promised you'd be home and you didn't even bother to call. It was our anniversary and you forgot and I was so down and so annoyed with you, and myself, that I just snapped and filed for divorce the next day. I admit I was stubborn and just couldn't go back on it."

"I understand, honestly I do. You're better off without me. But know this, Min. Anytime, anyplace, anywhere, I'll be there for you. Just say the word. Whatever you need, just call. As long as I have a signal that is. I'm starting in North Wales, and you know the reception can be iffy at campsites."

"Silly," giggled Min, radiating happiness and contentment. "Wow, what a year. You're so brave to do this."

"A year's a long time. Long enough for me to get my act together."

"More like untogether. You sold everything and are homeless!"

"But in a good way. And not anymore. I picked up the campervan the other day. It's loaded up and ready to go. Come take a look."

With a quizzical smile, Min nevertheless slipped on her shoes and followed me down the path and around the corner where the new, at least new to me, campervan was parked.

"It's orange and white."

"Sure is. Apparently it's a 1967 Volkswagen Type Two. A T1 split-screen window model with mostly original interior from when it was kitted out by Westfalia. Although I do get confused between T1 and T2 as different people seem to call them different things."

"I have no idea what you are talking about, Max, but it looks sweet."

"Sweet? It's awesome! It's got a roof you can raise so you can stand up, although I'm not sure if that is original, a three-quarter bed just big enough for two," I very unsubtly hinted, adding a wink in case she didn't get it, "and even a sink and a two-ring hob. There's a tiny fridge, sockets, and all that jazz. Come on, take the tour inside."

"I like it. It's retro, but very cool. It's a proper hippy van. I remember seeing these when I was a kid. Now everyone's got the modern versions or those great hulking campervans."

"I wanted something compact. Something that would be easy to drive and I could park anywhere. It's taking some getting used to as I only got it a few days ago, but it's pretty awesome, right?"

Anxious yipped his approval, tail wagging as he looked up to Min.

"Sorry, but no more biscuits. You've got a big trip, and you know you aren't good travelling on a full stomach," she told him, bending to scratch his ears.

Anxious bowed his head, nodding he understood.

"Well?" I asked.

"Yes, it's lovely. Perfect for you. Did you fit everything in?"

"Easy. It's got built-in cupboards, loads of storage, and I can't tell you how nice it is to just be travelling light anyway."

I opened the side doors to reveal the sixties and seventies interior from the various changes made over the years. There were modern touches too, but it looked the part and I loved it. It was like stepping back in time. Open to the front, the compact kitchen ran along the length of the far side, with units underneath that contained the gas bottle for the two-ring hob and fridge, water for the sink, and the small fridge itself that would take some getting used to, along with space for a limited amount of supplies and crockery.

To the right was the bench seat, covered in pinstriped retro material that'd seen better days but was holding up remarkably well.

"Look, there's a small pull-down seat here behind the passenger seat so you can perch there or use it as a handy table. Come in, let me show you the rest."

"It's very clean and tidy. And I love the old-fashioned feel."

I climbed up then held out a hand to help Min inside. With the roof already raised, there was plenty of room to stand. "Cool, eh? Look, you can pull these boards over above our heads and make a second bed. I think that might be a more modern addition though, not sure. The guy I bought it off talked for so long about the various models that I got confused, but I don't think these early VWs originally had the raised roof. But it's a nice little snug with the roof up. And the bench is what they call a 'Rock-n-Roll' bed, apparently. Let me show you."

I went through the instructions the seller had given, an excitable man in his fifties who was selling to upgrade to something bigger but was clearly in love with this old model. I pulled the bench flat, then dragged the board that acted as a surface in the rear and flipped it over. It locked into place in front of the flat bench and now there was a three-quarter bed filling most of the available floor space.

"Wow, that is cool, but it's a bit cramped."

"It's just for sleeping," I shrugged. "See?"

Anxious hopped onto the bed, turned in a circle several times, then plonked himself down and sighed.

"Looks like someone's already picked their spot," laughed Min.

"He does like to sleep on the bed," I admitted. "We'll be cosying up, you can guarantee that."

Min sat on the bed and stroked Anxious, a faraway look in her eyes. "Remember when we got him?"

"Of course I do."

"It was a sad time. We found out we couldn't have children and I was just so upset. I know I was hard to be with, and I know that's why you threw yourself into your work. I was the one to blame. I drove you away and you found comfort with cooking."

"No, don't blame yourself. I should have been there for you, but I wasn't."

"We were both to blame, then, let's admit that. I should have let you in, explained how utterly desolate I was, rather than push you away. But it is what it is. So, we decided to get a dog. What were we thinking?"

"We weren't. We thought it would fill the void."

"And he did, didn't he?"

"And then some," I chuckled, looking at Anxious curled up, so cute with his white bristly fur and patchwork brown, his slender form and wise eyes as he opened them to peer at us both.

"We went to that farm and there were eight of the tiniest little puppies you'd ever seen. He hid behind his mother when the others came over to play. Do you remember?"

"Every second of it. You said he seemed so anxious and that we should take him as he was really sweet. So we did."

"And he turned out to be the least anxious puppy in the world!" Min laughed, brushing away the tears, and smiling at him. "We definitely picked the wrong name for the little guy."

"We sure did. The moment he got home he was trouble. He destroyed everything, he bit my ankles every day for a month, but was great fun and has always been since. He misses you," I said, holding her gaze.

"Max, don't. I know what you're saying and I feel the same, but just don't, okay?"

"Okay. Right, come on you, get out of my house. We've got a deadline and it's a few hours to Rhyl. This old lady isn't the fastest, so we need to get going. I've got a packed lunch and hopefully we'll arrive before I need to eat it all. I want to explore once we get set up at the campsite."

"Are you going to stay at official sites every night?"

"No chance. Sometimes, yes, but that's the beauty of a campervan. There are lots of free spots where you can stay without charge. I bought a few books that list places that are legal to stay. And there is always the option to just park up somewhere out of the way and close the curtains. Did I show you them? Look." I pulled the tiny curtains that matched the upholstery across a window and said, "Ta-da."

Min clapped and smiled, warming my heart. "So cute."

We exited after I slid the bed back. Min said goodbye to Anxious then he went back inside and curled up on the passenger seat.

At the front of the VW, I shifted awkwardly from foot to foot, looking down, but Min failed to get the hint, so I bodged my idiot big reveal and pointed, clearing my throat so I didn't sound like a squeaky schoolboy trying to talk to a girl he fancied. Which, I absolutely did fancy this girl.

Min followed my finger and gasped as she locked eyes on the number plate.

"You utter muppet," she sighed, shaking her head but unable to hide her smile. "What were you thinking?"

"Pretty cool, eh? Cost a fortune, but it was worth it."

"You got a personalised number plate? You always said people who did that were just show-offs. That anyone who bought one had more money than sense."

"This is different. It isn't to show off. It's so you know."

"Know what?"

"That same as everything else, this is as much yours as mine. MAX M1N is the coolest number plate ever, right?"

"Oh yes, because nobody has ever made fun of the fact our names are Max and Min before, have they?" she pouted.

"Like I've always told you, it's fate. How could we possibly not be together with names like that? At least your surname isn't Effort." Min raised an eyebrow and I spluttered, "Um, yeah, yours actually is. I'm amazed you haven't changed it back to your maiden name."

"Why on earth would I? Who wouldn't just love to be called Min Effort? It's so average that nobody has ever commented on it." If sarcasm could ooze, then Min was standing in a puddle. More like a lake.

"Well, thank you for keeping it. I know you've had a lot of stick over the years because of it, but thanks."

"Actually, I prefer it now. And fine, the number plate is cool. Maybe I'll come join you for a day sometime on your trip. Just for the day," she added hurriedly. "So don't get any ideas."

"Wouldn't dream of it." I kept my smug smile to myself and tried to slow my fast-beating heart. Where there was hope, there was the dogged determination to never give up on what you knew was right. And the number plate may have been a rather foolish and expensive touch, but I knew Min would appreciate it.

"I like it. You big softy." Min stood on tiptoe and planted a warm, wet kiss on my cheek as I bent. Her five foot two petite frame at odds with my six foot one solid man body of pure hunky awesomeness, said nobody except me. Ever.

Min and Max Effort, the Little and Large duo. Our size difference, our names, and even our jobs—Min was a dietitian—so dissimilar to each other, yet somehow always having worked until things began to unravel. We'd had so much grief over it, but at least Min had missed out on the cruel jokes of children.

I forgave my parents many things, including insisting on always calling friends that came over "chums," but one thing I would resent them for until I got thrown in a hole when dead was for the utter madness that made them decide to call their one and only son Max when they damn well knew what their own surname was. It was like they got a temporary lobotomy while I was a baby, then someone decided to stuff most of the missing brain goop back in but leave a blank when anyone tried to explain maybe it wasn't the best idea for a name.

"Look after yourself," I said. "And call whenever you need to."

"Why would I need to?"

"Okay, just call me so I can hear your voice."

"Max." Min sighed and shook her head, but she wasn't cross, just very confused about our relationship. Hey, make that two of us. Anxious wasn't exactly free of the need for marriage counselling either.

"Sorry, I know you're a single lady of leisure now."

"Look who's talking."

"I'm no lady. You should hear about the bad things I've done," I winked, making her tut and smile.

"You know what I mean. You're the one gallivanting around the country in a seventies van. And I'm not a lady of leisure. I have my new job working with people who actually need the help, not rich people who refuse to stop eating unhealthy food. It's been good for me. I'm glad I gave up the old clients."

"Sixties. It's from sixty-seven."

"What?" asked Min, confused.

"The van. And if you want me to stay, you know I will."

Min put a hand to my chest and said, "Max, don't. We're divorced."

"I know. But call me anyway. Or, and you won't like it, I'll send you photos every day of all the castles and pubs we visit. We're going to visit lots of them, and I mean lots."

"I can imagine. Go on, off you go."

A minute later, I was watching Min wave to us from the rear-view mirror as we drove away and headed off for our first adventure.

"This will be awesome, Anxious," I told the excited Terrier as he sat on the passenger seat and watched the world go by. "Just you, me, and good times. Camping, cooking, and chilling out."

Anxious cocked his head and whined.

"It's hard, but she has her own life now. I know you miss her, but we have to accept that I blew it. But this should be incredible fun. Just what we need. First stop Rhyl, which is on the coast of North Wales, then we'll work our way west and follow the coast around until heading for Devon then Cornwall, and just see where the road takes us. How does that sound?"

Anxious barked excitedly.

"Good boy. Now, you rest, as it'll be hours until we get there and I need to focus on my driving. This gear stick is huge, and I still can't get used to this weird handbrake. It's like driving an old-fashioned bus and I need to concentrate."

Anxious nodded, then curled up and sighed as he closed his eyes. I put all thoughts of the past out of my mind and for the first time in years I actually felt truly relaxed. Carefree. Properly free. No shackles, no worry, no guilt, just me and Anxious and whatever the future held.

I had no plans to ever go back to my old life, as my days as a chef were over, and for good. I had money in the bank thanks to property investments when I was raking in the cash, with enough monthly income to cover the cost of travel, and having always adored the times I got to camp and travel with Min, mostly when I had forced time away from work for refurbishments or a change of job, I couldn't see myself buying a house again any time soon.

What was the point? Anxious and I were finally on our own, and as I drove north I realised something.

I was nervous.

Because although not truly alone, I wasn't with her. I finally accepted it. But I'd be buggered if I'd ever stop trying to right the wrongs I'd inflicted. Maybe by leaving I was giving her the space she needed to pursue a new life. Or maybe I was giving her some time to realise how wrong she'd been and how utterly awesome Max Effort was once he wasn't being an utter plonker.

Time would tell.

Chapter 2

Anxious stared at me in that way only Jack Russell Terriers can. At least, I assumed only they could stare with such a mix of love, hatred, longing, and patience. Having never had another Terrier, I was going by limited experience, but I got the gist.

"Yes, I'm hungry as well, but we ate our packed lunch an hour ago. You'll just have to wait until dinnertime. Guess what it is?"

Anxious whined and cocked his head, eyes never leaving mine.

"It's Cozido de grão. It's a Portuguese dish, although there are many variations on it," I lectured, Anxious keening to hear more about the intricacies of the rustic European dish's history. "Although, at heart, it's chickpeas and whatever meat you happen to have, I've got pork belly and sirloin and some authentic regional sausages."

Anxious' ears pricked up at the mention of sausage, and a long, gelatinous line of drool hung from his chops until he licked it away.

"Yes, sausages, and just a few vegetables." Anxious whinged at the mention of veg, but I knew his game and knew he'd wolf the lot the moment I served dinner. "But after today, we'll have to source whatever we can find as we travel about. Remember, it's one-pot cooking for dinner and nothing else. It'll be a challenge, but a rewarding one. All those years making fancy meals might mean I can cook up a storm, but I want basic food that'll fill me up and next to zero washing up. There's no dishwasher now, just a tiny sink and we have to remember to fill up the container for the water, so I'm keeping it simple."

Anxious glanced back into the rear of the campervan, just in case I'd happened to leave any sausages lying around, but he was out of luck.

Chuckling, my spirits high as I looked forward to our first night of life on the road, I stroked his head as he settled back down to dream of meat. Although no longer a chef with a job, I was certainly still a chef, but I was burned out, and sick of the precision fine-dining entailed. I needed to get back to basics, to enjoying food for what it was. Not garnishes and presentation, just a big bowl of something hearty and a fold-out chair to eat it from.

I took a turn and gasped.

"Look, it's the sea! Check out that water, Anxious."

Anxious sat and peered out of the window then barked for joy. He loved the beach as much as me, and adored playing chase on the sand or sprinting into the water, yapping and joyous as he retrieved a ball.

"This will be utterly awesome, buddy. You, me, fun, and freedom. We should be there soon. About half an hour according to the directions." I tore my eyes from the sparkling water, the sun still high on a perfect June day. We had the whole summer to get used to our new life before the weather changed and we'd have to spend more time under cover. But the forecast was for a long heatwave the likes of which the UK had never seen before, and I intended to make the most of what might be a once-in-a-lifetime promise of high temperatures and almost zero chance of rain for at least a month, maybe more if the weatherman was to be believed. Not that you could ever trust them. They may have had fancy graphs and lots of computers, but I knew they still just made it up and crossed their fingers.

As the road switched back and we lost the view, Anxious settled down and I focused on my driving. We were soon enveloped in deep shade where the narrowing road was carved into a steep cliff covered in moss and ferns and the view was hidden by rhododendrons and hydrangeas fronting coastal properties overlooking the sea.

The map on my phone gave directions, but I missed it as we were rocking out to an eighties mix tape I'd been given by my parents and found when I cleared out my stuff from the house and had kept along with the box of tapes for some reason. It was serendipity, as now I had unlimited sounds to listen to on the old cassette player that worked perfectly even if the speakers were rather tinny.

Duran Duran's *Planet Earth* morphed into Dexy's Midnight Runners screaming about Eileen and the good mood was contagious. Maybe I'd buy a pair of dungarees and get a red bandana, rather than just wearing cut-off jeans and a black vest. Min would have a fit if she saw me in anything but my usual outfit, which mostly consisted of jeans and T-shirt, but with my new look of long hair and beard, I bet I could pull it off. Why wouldn't a thirty-three-year-old six foot one man with a tight body look awesome in eighties dungarees?

I shook my head and smiled, my mood buoyant as I anticipated setting up at the campsite and enjoying the evening. We'd go for a walk on the beach, then I'd let dinner bubble away for a few hours and eat whenever it was ready. No timetable here, no rush orders, no sweaty, noisy kitchen or staff having a meltdown. No need to even wipe the plate after serving it up. I'd just slosh it on and splashes be damned.

Another turn, and we were on the track to the campsite. Golygfa Maes was the name of the Welsh campsite. Unpronounceable for anyone not from around these parts. A quaint, quiet place that catered to those wishing to get away from it all. Set a mile from the coast up a winding lane, it was a working farm with a few fields for camping or campervans, but with little in the way of amenities beyond a shower block and somewhere to hook up for electric. I needed the toilet block, but could most likely do without the electric hook-up if I ran into any issues.

I'd bit the bullet and bought a new leisure battery for the Volkswagen camper, run from a solar panel on the roof, but if needed I could charge it up. Being sensible, I'd also splurged on a large portable power bank that could be plugged into or used to charge via USB cables. It was at a hundred percent, and if the reviews were to be believed it would last me weeks before I had to bother charging it. It meant I could use my laptop outside, or even hook it up to the battery if the sun wasn't shining.

It would be a steep learning curve—I knew nothing about campervan life beyond what I'd devoured on Youtube—#vanlife—and I was still getting used to the quirks of the 1967 VW T1, but that was the whole point. Adventure. I didn't need to know all there was to know about VW campervans, all I needed to know was that I wanted this life and would work the rest out as I went along.

The road twisted and turned, and the glorious day vanished once more beneath a tunnel of trees that closed in from all sides. Lush and dense, the small woodland led directly to the campsite.

Signs confirmed we were heading the right way, so I turned off the map and cranked up the Human League, singing *Don't You Want Me* at the top of my lungs.

Anxious howled along, either out of pity or to shame me into silence, as I slowed to a crawl to go over the speed bumps without bottoming out the delicate undercarriage of what was, after all, a vehicle much older than me.

We bounced about in our seats and I grumbled about the lack of suspension as we navigated the humps, but the lane was so narrow anyway that I wouldn't have been going much faster. I prayed nobody would come the other way, as I was yet to reverse, and the gear stick was more like trying to wrangle a Rubik's Cube in the dark with one hand than the conventional gears I was used to.

It was so gloomy now that I could hardly see a thing, the cover was so dense, so I panicked as I searched for the headlights, then found the correct position and the way ahead lit up.

I slammed on the brakes, putting an arm out to stop Anxious from snapping the dog seatbelt taut and damaging his neck, but got a nasty burn on my chest as my own seatbelt snapped tight, the one concession to modern laws meaning that both seats and the rear bench had modern safety features.

My heart hammered in my chest as I squinted out of the split windscreen at the mysterious mound in the road that might, or might not have been, a speed bump. Something had made me stop, and now my mind was catching up with my eyes.

Anxious whined, so I rubbed his head and told him he was a good boy. He wagged, but I could tell his heart wasn't in it, and his nose was dilating rapidly as he sniffed, trying to uncover a scent my own inferior nostrils failed to pick up on.

I undid my seatbelt, then his, turned off the engine, then opened the door and jumped out. Anxious joined me and stood by my side, hackles raised, growling as his eyes locked on the misshapen "speed bump" in the road.

"Who am I kidding? This isn't a speed bump." I glanced around nervously at the trees. Twisted, looming sentinels perfect for a mad axe-man to hide behind then jump out and attack once his quarry stopped to remove whatever he'd placed in the road as a cunning barrier.

Was it a fallen tree? A rolled-up old mattress? A blanket? Maybe a tourist had lost their roof box or tent? I cursed myself for not driving a little closer as the campervan's headlights weren't strong enough to light it up properly. But I didn't think starting it right now was a good idea for some reason, so approached slowly with Anxious by my side, his fur now on end, his growl deepening as we tried to make out what exactly was blocking our way.

Staying to one side so the headlights could provide as much light as possible, I shuffled forward, eyes darting, feeling freaked-out and vulnerable. I began to sweat even though it was cool and damp. The tinny beats of Lionel Richie singing about dancing on the ceiling reached me through the open door of the VW.

"Lionel Richie, will you shut up for a minute?" I hollered, my voice echoing back at me. "And what was he even going on about?" I muttered, marching forward before my nerves got the better of me.

"It's just a tent," I laughed, sighing with relief as the mess of green fabric took on a recognisable form. Guy ropes and tent poles stuck out of the bundle of waterproof fabric at weird angles, making it look like an insect drawn by a child studiously ignoring correct anatomy. The dark lump rippled as a breeze swept through the tunnel of trees, causing me to shiver. It was hard to believe that out from under the canopy the sun was shining and it was a beautiful day.

Anxious approached cautiously, still growling, eyes glued on the tent.

"It's alright, it's just a tent. I bet it fell off someone's roof or something. You going to give me a hand to move it?"

Anxious looked from me to the densely rolled tent, most likely a large model that weighed a lot, and lifted a paw as if to tell me I was on my own here.

"Suit yourself. Maybe go and tell Lionel Richie to give it a rest then?"

I bent to grab the tent, but Anxious barked loudly and took a step away, head down, tail still, growling through bared teeth.

"What's got into you? Bit spooked too, eh?" I laughed, ruffling his head as he gingerly approached. "Go have a pee or something. I bet you need one." Anxious was going nowhere, though, and pressed tight against my side. "Suit yourself."

I grabbed the end of the tent, and braced, expecting it to weigh a bit but sure it would be easy enough to drag out of the way. I'd load it up in the campervan and see what the campsite owner suggested in terms of disposal.

The tent didn't budge. I heaved, straining, but it still wouldn't move.

"Must have some luggage caught in it. Or maybe a few dozen bricks by the feel of it." Grumbling, I tried to sort out the poles, and make sense of where the opening was. Having finally found an end, I dealt with the mass of knots from the guy ropes—it was almost as if they'd been tied together like this on purpose, but who packed a tent this way?—then began to unroll the tangled material.

Under the confusion of the outer layer, it seemed to be rolled up compactly, yet not a big tent like I'd expected, so I pushed the roll with my feet, shielding my eyes as I was facing the headlights now, the tent little but shadow, but it still felt solid and was hard to budge. There was nothing for it, so I got down on hands and knees.

Anxious nervously came beside me, then sniffed, and glanced at me. He bent, and I noticed several smears on the fabric, which he licked at until they were gone.

"Taste nice, does it?" I asked, shaking my head. "You can't be so hungry you want to lick a tent."

Anxious sniffed around the fabric again, finding several sweet spots and licking them clean, but then his hackles rose again and he backed away.

I heaved against the material, pushing it over and over until the tent unravelled. I got closer and closer to the campervan, then with a final heave, whatever was weighing it down came free and rolled away a little down the potholed road.

Laying on a crumpled mess of bloody tent fabric was the body of a man. His head was shaved to disguise his baldness, the scalp covered in blood, as was his face and bushy ginger beard. He appeared to be in his twenties, but I was no expert, and wore nothing but his birthday suit. He was toned, slender, and had deep tan marks indicating he'd spent plenty of time wearing nothing but a pair of above-the-knee shorts and a T-shirt, weather permitting, like he was a surfer or something.

His body glistened where he'd most likely been sweating under the tent, the trapped moisture now running in rivulets of red that tracked between his ribs. His body was a mass of bruises, and I scrambled back in shock even though I was mesmerised. I simply couldn't look away as I watched a bead of red at his forehead slide down past his eye and wander like a tear across his cheek, along his neck, and pool below his Adam's Apple in the little hollow there.

He wore a basic waterproof watch, but other than that he was devoid of any jewellery. I noted a birthmark on his right side, an earthy blotch even through the tan. His eyes were open, staring up at a sliver of blue sky through the canopy.

My stomach heaved but I refused to puke. I'd already utterly contaminated what was clearly a crime scene; last thing I wanted to do was cause more damage.

Anxious was barking from behind me, so I soothed him and suggested he go back to the VW. He raced off and launched himself inside, so I heaved to my feet and followed him, skirting the body widely, unable to look at the poor man again.

I reached inside to get my phone, not surprised to find there was no signal under the trees. Recalling the website for the campsite, I cursed as I remembered they said the phone signal was problematic and unreliable, so there was no point just walking out from the cover and trying again. The best bet was to drive to the campsite and tell them what I'd found so they could use a landline if the signal was down.

Grossed out, but knowing the poor man deserved at least some respect, I rolled the tent over him just the once, then with a surprising amount of effort I dragged him to the narrow verge and onto the grass then bunched the rest of the tent over him so it was safe from other vehicles.

Dazed, I got back into the VW and started the engine then floored it and tore through the rest of the forest, thankfully not encountering any more speed bumps.

We emerged into glorious bright sunshine, and I gasped for the joy of being alive and for the sky. Before us lay a beautiful sight. Lush fields, animals grazing, tents pitched, campervans parked, and a squat, lichen-encrusted stone farmhouse with assorted outbuildings, some derelict. Where the cliffs dropped off, the sea glistened with the promise of warm water and pleasant strolls along the beach.

Boats bobbed on the still water; all I felt was the churning of my stomach as my head filled with the ghastly scene I'd just uncovered.

I opened the gate, drove through, then hopped out and closed it behind me. Feeling weary, I went up the short path to the farmhouse and paused outside the door. The paint had long ago been eroded by sun and salt-laden wind, leaving a pale silver mottled with green behind. It couldn't have been more than five feet high, almost as wide, a typical cottage style where the buildings hunkered down low to avoid the worst of the weather.

Heavy of heart, I knocked.

Chapter 3

Dogs yipped from inside; someone shouted and they fell silent. Footsteps came closer, then the door was flung open almost as though the owner had a grudge against it and a hunched figure still had to duck to exit the cottage. An old man wearing blue overalls with broad shoulders, thinning hair a shock of white, with a tanned face—more lined than the shirts I'd stuffed into any available nook and cranny in the campervan—glared at me with dark eyes from under the bushiest eyebrows I'd ever seen. Even with his severe curvature of the spine, he matched me in height, and must have been almost seven-feet tall before age and his condition took its cruel toll.

"Who are you? Did you book?" he grumbled in a Welsh accent so thick it took several moments for my brain to decode the words. There was a singsong lilt to his voice, the same for all true Welshmen whose first language wasn't English.

"Hi, yes. The name's Max. I booked for four nights. An electric hookup if you have one. But that's not why I'm here."

"Why are you here then?" he asked, glaring. "You booked from today, but you aren't here to camp? Is this one of those hidden camera shows?" He frowned as he glanced around, like maybe there was a team hidden in the bushes.

"Of course I'm here to camp. I wouldn't be here otherwise," I said, confused.

He leaned forward and stared hard, his dark brown eyes impossible to read. "Are you trying to be funny, city boy? This what passes for a joke in your posh fancy apartment, is it? We don't take kindly to people making fun of us around here. Maybe you need to go home and sit in your penthouse and stare smugly at your gold taps and diamond-encrusted table."

"Huh? No, look, let's start again. Yes, I'm Max, and yes, I want to stay, but I found a body in the road. Just back in the woods."

"A body you say?" He lifted the biggest hand I'd ever seen in my life, like a shovel with fingers, and rubbed at his stubble. "Ah," he brightened, "you mean a badger? Shame, they're such beautiful creatures. It's why we have the speed bumps. People should know better than to race their fancy city tractors over them."

"City tractors?"

"You know, people who buy a brand new Range Rover when they never leave town. Bit pointless if you ask me."

"Right, sure. It wasn't a badger. It was a man. A naked man. Wrapped in a tent. He was in the road. I unrolled it and found him."

"A man you say?" he mused, again stroking his chin.

"A man," I agreed.

Anxious barked his agreement, then, incongruously, rubbed against the farmer's leg.

He looked down, spied Anxious, and his whole demeanour softened. "Well, look here. A Jack Russell! Who's a good boy?" With bones creaking, he bent stiffly and patted Anxious, nearly flattening him.

Anxious just wagged and licked his lips. Maybe the old guy smelled of sausages.

"I haven't got a signal, so couldn't phone the police. Do you have a landline?"

"We aren't Spanish," he growled, giving me the evil eye.

"No, I don't suppose you are," I said, having no idea what that meant. "So, you do have a landline?" I encouraged. I just got another glare. "Can you phone the police? Tell them?"

"You sure it's a dead man?"

"It looked like one. He had a penis, if that's any help."

The farmer's head shot up. He studied me for the longest time, then burst out laughing, hearty and loud, startling me and Anxious.

"What do I need with a penis?" he hissed. Then he tugged at his ear, thought for a moment, and admitted, "I might want to rephrase that. But I definitely don't think it will help."

"No, I suppose not. No help at all."

I stood there feeling like a right lemon until he got his breath back and said, "I like you. But you know all male mammals have a penis, don't you? You aren't that much of a city boy are you?"

"I'm no city boy! I've spent more of my life in the country than in town. I love the outdoors and the wilds, and I always worked at restaurants in the countryside where we used the freshest produce direct from the ground." Damn, I even sounded like a city boy to my own ears now.

"Oh, you're one of them."

"One of what?" I asked, confused by this old fella and his ways.

"A fancy pants, hoity toity chef who serves you three bites of food for a main meal and charges you fifty quid. I bet you served ice-cream that tasted like sausage and sausage that tasted like ice-cream. Liked to be gracious enough to offer a mouthful of food on a deconstructed plate and charge fifty quid for it, I bet."

"Make that sixty," I admitted, shoulders slumping. "But I packed all that in. It's one-pot cooking on a fire or in the old VW from now on," I said, indicating the campervan parked in the weedy yard.

The farmer glanced over and whistled. "Nice. All original?" he snapped, daring me to admit otherwise.

"Most of it. I think there were some changes in the seventies and I'm not sure the roof is original as it folds up, but the interior's the same as the sixties."

"Excellent. Sixty-three or seven?"

"Sixty-seven splittie," I said confidently, hoping it would sound like I knew what I was on about.

"With a cassette player, or did you rip it out and put a CD player in?"

"Um, I don't think people even use CD players now. It's digital streaming. But no, it's a cassette player."

"Good lad," he grunted. "Dai is the name. Dai Roberts."

"Max Effort."

"What is?"

"My name?"

"Very funny. No need to take the proverbial."

"No, it really is. I hate my parents, and they clearly had it in for me when they named me. I think they did a Johnny Cash on me. May as well have called me a man named Sue."

"Never trust your parents," he said, nodding sagely. "They get up to all sorts. It shouldn't be allowed."

"What, parents?"

"You trying to be funny again?" he scowled, switching between agreeable and angry so often I couldn't keep up.

"No, what's with you?"

"Just messing with you, lad. Come on, you better show me this so-called body. The one with the penis."

"It's really there."

"The penis?"

"And the rest of him. We should call it in. Get the police out."

"We will, lad, as soon as I know you aren't pulling my leg. Speaking of legs, can you walk?"

What was with this guy? "Yes, I can walk. See." I pointed down at the two long bits beneath my waist that had Crocs on the end, hoping it was proof enough, but he was having none of it.

"Let's see them in action then."

I walked in a circle, then stood in front of him and asked, "Good enough?"

"Aye, it'll do, lad. Let's go take a peek at your," he air quoted me, "'corpse' then."

"Come on, Anxious, let's go and show Dai the dead man."

"Wait! Did you call your dog Anxious?"

"Yes, that's his name. It's a long story, and he isn't, but that's his name."

"Sounds about right," he agreed amiably, then reached back into the house, grabbed a gnarled stick, and pointed towards the road. "Let's go. To the penis!" he shouted.

Dai was fast, his bow legs and hunched back in no way hindering his speed. He marched off like he had a sheep to rescue from the hillside, hardly using his stick at all. Anxious and I caught up once our bewilderment had settled into mere confusion, and we were soon back in the gloom of the trees. We came to the spot several minutes later, where I stopped and glanced at Dai.

"He's in there. I had to drag him from the road as he was in the way."

"Aye, don't want the poor bugger getting squished. Won't be good for visitors if they have goop all over their wheels."

"No, I suppose not. Well, now can we call the police?"

"Let me see. I might recognise him. We're busy, but not so busy I don't know whose been staying and who left recently." Dai pointed with his stick, possibly in case I was thinking of some other corpse wrapped in a tent.

"I don't suppose it matters now, as I've already contaminated everything. Anxious kept licking the tent too."

"What, peed on it all, did you?" he asked us both.

Anxious whined and took a step back, looking rather guilty although I was sure he hadn't.

"Why on earth would I do that?"

"I heard the stories about you posh city folks. Especially the chefs. You love to pee on stuff." He got right up in my face, eyes studying me like I was about to pee on him, and I felt my panic rising.

This dude was seriously weird. Maybe it was him. Maybe he killed his guests and this was just the latest, and now I'd led him back into the woods so he could kill me and wrap me in a tent. I moved away and snapped, "I didn't pee on anyone."

"Ever?" he asked, glaring from beneath his wobbling eyebrows.

"Ever," I insisted. "Although, yeah, there was this time at the beach when I was twelve and my dad got stung by a jellyfish. He said it would help the pain."

"Did it work?"

"No, but I didn't really need to go, so it wasn't very much."

"True."

"What?"

"Nothing. Get on with it. I haven't got all day."

"Got plans, have you?" I asked brightly.

"No."

"Oh." It didn't take long to unroll the tent, even with the mess of poles and guy ropes, leaving the poor man exposed.

We stared down at him, and I noted that although there was plenty of blood, there didn't seem to be any visible wound. Surely to be covered in it, he must have an injury somewhere? Maybe on his back, or his head, and it had pooled in the tent after he was rolled up? That was for the police to figure out, not me.

"He's definitely dead," noted Dai.

"For sure. So, the landline?"

"Aye, let's go give the local copper a call. Bethan's new to the job, but a good girl. She'll be right over. Bet this'll make her day."

"Girl?"

"The opposite of a man. The ones without the dangly bits. What is wrong with you?"

"I meant she sounds young. Can she handle this? Why would it make her day? And why are you so obsessed with genitalia. It's starting to freak me out."

"My granddaughter is a fine policewoman, I'll have you know. And it will make her day as this will be her first real murder."

"Oh, right. Is she good at her job?"

Dai spun on me and grabbed my T-shirt in his disconcerting fist. "What you trying to say? You saying she isn't up to solving this?"

"No, of course not. But won't there be detectives? Forensics? And, er, do we have coroners in this country, or is that on TV shows? What are they called?"

"Your guess is as good as mine, lad," said Dai, smoothing down my shirt then patting my chest before smiling. "Come on, let's go give Bethan a call." Whistling, he marched back towards the campsite.

Anxious and I exchanged an utterly confounded look, so I wrapped up the body without looking too hard then hurried after him.

By the time we arrived, Dai was exiting the farmhouse looking happy. "She's on her way. She's very excited," he said, grinning.

"Should she be?"

"On her way?" he frowned.

"Excited," I sighed.

"Of course. It's a big deal. Don't belittle a murder. Right," he rubbed his hands together, "let's get you settled in. You can park anywhere in the fields you like. I don't book spaces. There are electric hookups dotted about so take your pick. It's not peak season yet, so we're half empty, but it'll get busier tomorrow as it's the weekend. The sunset is the best from the top field, but it's further to the toilets. No pooing in the hedge," he warned, wagging a finger.

"Wasn't planning on."

"I don't blame you. Off you go then. Enjoy your stay. Oh, did you pay?"

"Yes, online. For four nights, remember?"

"That's grand. Any problems, come find me. I'm always around. I expect Bethan will want to have a word, what with the dead naked man, and no doubt the idiot detectives will be along, but have a nice stay, and enjoy yourself." Dai spun, marched inside, slammed the door shut, and shouted at his dogs to stop barking.

Anxious and I shook our heads, then went back to the campervan. With the doors closed, I turned to him and asked, "Was it me, or was that guy weird?" Anxious just sat there. "Thought so. He didn't seem bothered about a body wrapped in a tent just outside his property. I wonder what happened? Who would do such a thing? Keep your eyes open, and don't trust anyone. For all we know, the murderer is still on the campsite."

Suddenly it hit me. The killer really might still be here. Or lurking somewhere close by. What if I'd been spotted? What if it was me next? No, things like that didn't happen in real life. Whatever the reason why that man was killed, it didn't mean I'd be stripped and bludgeoned then stuffed into the rear of the campervan next to my fold-out chair. It was most likely an argument gone wrong over drug deals or gangster stuff. No matter that we were in sleepy Rhyl, there were bad sorts everywhere, so we were safe. Right?

I drove along the track then up to the top field where the short grass was edged by a hedge before giving way to the wilds of the hills behind. Dai was right, there was plenty of space with loads of electric hook-ups, but the best spot was right up in the far corner where it was the quietest and most level, and I didn't need the power for just a few days as I planned on using as little electricity as possible. The evenings were long, it was light until gone nine, and cooking was by gas, so I parked up on level ground at the top of the hill, made sure the handbrake was firmly on, then got out, opened up the side doors, gave Anxious a bowl of water, swigged some myself, then put the kettle on.

I turned to stare out to sea, and managed to relax a little. It was beautiful here, exactly what I'd wished for. And then it hit me. I wasn't just staying for a few days then going back to the grind. No sweating away in a kitchen, feeling stressed and longing for something different. This was my life now. I could do anything, go anywhere, and take my time about it too.

The start had been horrendous, and no doubt I'd be asked a lot of questions, but this was certainly turning out to be quite an adventure already. I pulled out my phone, excited to message Min and tell her what had been going on, but maybe that wasn't such a clever idea. She'd only worry, and like she said, we weren't married anymore. I should give her some space. I'd also promised to message Mum and Dad, as they were hardly over the moon about me leaving, but there was no signal anyway, so that was one problem sorted.

I faffed about in the campervan, trying to familiarise myself with things, get a system going, but I knew that would take time and for now I'd just have to make do as best I could. I had water, I had coffee, I had milk, and even a pack of biscuits, so I made my first cuppa on the gas stove, set out my camping chair, and kicked back and enjoyed the sunny afternoon.

People came and went from the campsite. Off on trips or arriving for the weekend. Only a few though, as like Dai said, tomorrow would be a busier day and we weren't in peak season yet. I made a mental note of the tents and campervans already here, just in case it would help the police. Mostly, I was lost to the beauty of the place, the water glistening, the sense of being part of something, of the real world, perfect for all its imperfections. For the first time in as long as I could remember, I felt at peace.

Chapter 4

"Mate. Mate," whispered a voice.

I opened my eyes to find a grinning man staring down at me. He wore nothing but cut-off denim shorts, with a healthy tan and sun-streaked hair. He was barefoot and I instantly took to him. I guessed him to be late twenties, but I was as good at guessing ages as I was at speaking Welsh, so he might have been sixteen or approaching forty.

"Hi," I said, yawning.

"Sorry, did I wake you? Um, yeah, I know I did, because you were snoring. Sorry," he grinned cheerily.

"No problem. I must have nodded off. Wow, it's warm."

"Awesome, eh? It's going to be the best summer ever. I can't wait. Me and the girlfriend have this awesome trip planned around the coast, and we're following the waves. There are some amazing places to surf off the coast. It's no Cornwall, but we'll get there eventually. No hurry, right?"

This guy was a chatterbox, but I liked him. "Sounds perfect. In fact, I've got the same route planned too. Minus the surfing."

"Oh, man, you gotta surf. It's the best. You think this feels like freedom? Wait until you ride the waves. It's like flying."

"I can imagine. What can I do for you?"

"Just came over to say hi." The man kicked at the grass with a dirty foot, then parted his blond hair to reveal shining blue eyes and a wicked grin. "Okay, that's a lie. And no offence, but I saw the VW and had to come see. Original sixty-seven, right?"

"Yes. And the interior is original Westfalia, too, or so I was told. I'm not sure, and there's been some changes to the inside, but most of it's how it was out of the factory."

"That's awesome, dude. No way. That's us down there." He pointed to an almost identical VW campervan but in red rather than orange, and a woman waved back up at us. "Ours is original too, although some pleb swapped out a few things and the bumpers and a few other bits and pieces aren't right, but yours, man, it looks like it would have when it was first out. So cool."

"Thanks, but it isn't down to me. I only bought it recently, and this was just how it came. The previous owner restored a lot, but he said he bought it off someone who'd had it since new, so I'm only the third person to own it."

"That's incredible! So you aren't a VW buff?" he asked, hope in his eyes.

"Not really. I always liked the look of them, but I wouldn't know the difference between the various models," I admitted.

"That doesn't matter. You'll be a convert soon enough. Mind if I take a look inside?"

"No, of course not." I got up and frowned at Anxious who remained where he was curled up by the chair. "Some guard dog you are?" I grumbled.

Anxious just wagged his tail then closed his eyes. To be fair, I guess he just knew this man wasn't a threat so stayed put.

The side doors were open to let the air flow through with the windows down, and the man turned and frowned as we stood there.

"What? Is there a problem?"

"A problem?" he squealed. "This is utterly awesome! Mate, do you know what you have here?"

"An old VW campervan?" I offered, that being the extent of my knowledge.

"You, my friend, have a slice of history. It's immaculate. Don't change a thing," he warned.

"I won't. But look, the socket outlets aren't original, they've been added, and there's solar and batteries and seatbelts. And the roof opens up."

"That doesn't matter. That's just sensible stuff, but the look, the fittings, the important stuff is all here. The original sink, the doors, even the hinges, and the spare seat, it's all intact. Bet you love it, right?"

"Actually," I admitted, "I haven't spent the night in it yet. This is my first day, and it's been a weird one."

"How so?"

I was in two minds whether or not to tell him about the body, but then figured why not? And wasn't it better if he and his girlfriend knew so they could take whatever precautions they felt necessary?

I explained what had happened, and his eyes grew wider the more I told. When I was finished, he sucked in air through his teeth then slapped me on the back, smiled, and said, "Don't worry about it, man."

"Don't worry? Someone was murdered."

"Yeah, but it's not our business. Stay out of it. Things like that happen now and then. We've been on the road for three years, and something nasty happens occasionally. Not serial killer nasty, but you gotta keep in mind that sometimes campsites and out-of-the-way places are where the bad guys hang out. It's private, and they can see who's coming. You get drug dealers, all kinds of criminals, but chill out, it's safe most of the time. Just a few dodgy characters along the way. It makes for an adventure, right?" he said, beaming.

"I guess. I hadn't really thought about anything like this happening."

"The police will get it sorted. Leave them to it. Don't get embroiled."

"I won't. How could I?"

He shrugged, then said, "I'm Mickey, and my lady is Sue."

"Max," I said, shaking hands.

"Well now, Max, let me give you a few tips for your first night."

"Sure, that would be great."

"Rule number one of these beauties is ensure you always make your bed well before you plan to sleep, and always while it's still light, and fold it away as soon as you get up. You'll want the space. Never let your water get too low for the sink or for drinking, and always keep it separate. Don't drink from the tap as the original water container is so old. I assume you have a new one for drinking?"

"Yes, bought it the other day. A large container in the back."

"Good man. What else? Oh yeah, do your dishes straight away, and boil the kettle for hot water. Don't try to do it with cold. It doesn't work."

"I know. I used to be a chef, so I know about hot water."

"That's cool. What about heating and staying cool? You got an air-conditioning unit?"

"Actually, yes. The previous owner said it would be almost unbearable otherwise, and if I'm out in the winter I'd need the heat."

"He was right, you will. Make sure you use it. But keep the precious one ventilated as much as you can or it'll get damp."

"Thanks for the tips."

"You're welcome. The main thing is to enjoy it. The open road is a wondrous thing. We love it. We work from our laptops and can go anywhere we want. Digital nomads. It's awesome. But watch your cash. It's easy to burn through the money if you stay at campsites every night. We do one or two nights a week to charge up and get water, have showers, that kind of thing, but make use of free places to stay."

"That's what I was thinking. I got a few books that list the free pub car parks and other places you can stay for a night, so will use them."

"Yeah, good thinking. But even better is stealth parking. Don't do it anywhere that you're causing a nuisance, but out-of-the-way lay-bys or quiet spots are ideal. You shouldn't have any bother. It isn't quite legal all the time, but we've never had a problem as long as you never leave any mess and keep quiet."

"Thanks, and that's certainly an option. I don't want to cause trouble for anyone though."

"Yeah, I get it. We mostly do it to save money or if we find a cool spot, but it isn't for everyone. Oh, and don't be surprised if you get lots of people coming to take a look at the old girl. She's a real beauty."

"Thanks, and I appreciate the tips."

Mickey nodded, then padded down the hill to his girlfriend and they began to talk. Their voices rose as Mickey gesticulated, but then they went inside the campervan and the door slid closed. I guess he was in trouble for something. Maybe she'd made a drink, or thought I didn't want to be disturbed.

My stomach began to rumble, so even though it was very early I decided I'd better think about making dinner. It needed a few hours to cook slowly, and I had to brown off the meat and the onions first before letting it simmer, so I'd best make a start.

Back in the van, I began pulling out what I'd need, the prized possession my large cast-iron cooking pot that I'd owned for years. Top of the range and guaranteed for life, it had seen many meals already, but now it was about to embark on a new life. My main pot every evening. I salivated at the thought of finally being able to eat whilst in no hurry, no desire to watch the TV, check email, or wolf my food to get back to work. I had all the time in the world, and I intended to enjoy every minute of it.

"Hello?" came a female voice from outside the campervan as I began to get things sorted.

With a longing look at the onions and the chopping board, I turned to find a very pretty and very young police officer standing there.

She jumped back, cheeks reddening, as I ducked to exit the van.

"Was it you?" she hissed, eyes wide.

"Was what me?"

"Are you the murderer?" she gasped.

"Me? No. I'm the one who found the body."

"Because you killed him?"

"No, stop saying that. Are you Bethan?"

"You know my name?" she shrieked, her pretty hazel eyes widening.

"Yes, Dai told me. Why are you freaking out?"

"Because of that!" Bethan's eyes drifted down and I realised I was clutching my prized dicing knife. It was very sharp, and gleamed in the sun, the Japanese steel razor sharp.

"Oh, sorry. I was about to prepare dinner." I stepped in and placed the knife on the counter then hopped back out and smiled, hopefully putting her at ease. "Better?"

Bethan sighed then smiled, her smooth cheeks rounding. "Yes. And sorry about that. You surprised me."

"So, any clues yet?" I joked, not expecting this very young woman to even know the full story. Her uniform was as crisp and fresh as she was, like it was brand new. She had her dark hair tied back in a loose bun, although her wavy locks had other ideas and were making a break for freedom. The bouncy curls couldn't hide the softness of her face or the keenness in her eyes reserved for those yet to be jaded by the harsher side of life.

"Just one."

"Oh, what's that?" I asked, surprised.

"The body in the tent. Is it horrid? Grandad said you discovered it. What was it like?"

"Haven't you looked yet?"

"No. I got the call from Dai, so dashed right over. In case you haven't noticed, this area isn't a hotbed of murder. Best I've ever had is a few drunken lads outside Wetherspoons."

"Oh, are you new to the force?"

"Less than a year, and I got given the local farms. We have a proper big station in Rhyl, but I'm stationed in the village to serve the local community and most of my call-outs are for lost sheep or arguing farmers. They get pretty worked up when it comes to boundary disputes and they all own shotguns. None of them have ever used them though," she said morosely, clearly keening for some action.

"Then this is your lucky day, I guess," I said brightly.

"Yes, it is! Now, can you show me the body, please?" Bethan was itching to go take a look, me not so much.

"Do I need to come with you? It's just up in the woods by the roadside. I've already seen it twice, and it's pretty gross."

"I might need assistance, sir," snapped Bethan, falling into strict police constable mode. It wasn't very convincing.

"Why not take Dai?"

"Aw, please? You've met him, so you know what he's like. He likes to joke around too much, and he's always messing with people. He's a real sweetie, but he won't take anything seriously. He needs to, as this will not be good for the campsite. Not at all. He doesn't understand, but it might be disastrous."

I could imagine Dai being called many things, but joker and sweetie certainly wouldn't make it onto my list. "He didn't seem the type to joke around."

"He likes to wind the tourists up, act sullen then friendly. It disconcerts them, but he reckons it's good for business. Says everyone that comes here will go away remembering him, and he's right, they do."

"But do they come back?"

"Some of them do," Bethan chuckled, her eyes twinkling.

"I like you, Bethan, so okay, let's go. But shouldn't you wait for the detectives to arrive? What about coroners and forensics and all that stuff? To be honest, I'm not sure how it works, but won't there be lots of police at the crime scene?"

"Soon enough, yes. Maybe an hour or so. Which means it doesn't give us much time. We need to get a move on before we get crowded out and I'm left doing the rubbish jobs."

"We? What's with the we?"

"You found the body, so you know more than anyone else. I'm sure you want the killer found, so it's best if we take a look before the place is packed."

"You want to solve this, don't you?" I asked, watching her squirm before she squared her shoulders and met my eyes.

"Of course I do! I want to show that I'm a proper police officer and deserve to be given some decent crimes to solve. One day," she moved closer and confided, "I want to be a detective. I'll start at DC then move on to DI. That's detective constable and detective inspector. Real crimes. But I'm stuck breaking up old men arguing over sheep and the height of hedges or whose turn it is to dig out the overflow ditches. So let's go!" she snapped, making Anxious jump up and trot over then sit by her and await further instructions.

"Yes, ma'am," I said, hiding my smile.

"Right." With a nod, Constable Bethan turned and marched away.

"Hey, what do I call you? What's your title?"

"Police Constable Bethan Jones," she said as Anxious and I caught her up. "But Jones is about as common as sheep around here, so everyone calls me BJ."

"They call you BJ?" I asked, gobsmacked.

"Yes, short for Bethan Jones."

"Oh, right, yes, of course."

"Why? What did you think it stood for?"

"Um, just that, obviously," I said hurriedly. "But do you mind if I call you Bethan?"

"Of course not. No need to be formal. We're a team."

"Are we?" This was the first I was hearing of this. I just wanted to make my Portuguese stew and sit in my chair whilst it bubbled away. Maybe have a beer. Maybe two. Possibly three. This was not the first day I'd envisioned. Not at all.

Back across the field, I spied Dai waving to a scruffy man in his fifties standing beside a battered brown Volvo. He looked bewildered, and shook his shoulder length lank brown hair before rolling up the sleeves of a brown shirt that matched his brown corduroys. He got into the colour-coded car, started it with a splutter of fumes, then drove towards us.

"Doesn't look like the camping type," I noted, thinking no more of it.

"Might be a suspect," said Bethan keenly.

"You think?" This woman really was eager.

As the Volvo slowly came parallel to us, Bethan held up a hand and stepped in front of the vehicle. The driver stopped, then pulled on the handbrake with a grating squeal.

Bethan walked around to the driver's side and the man leaned out of the window. Anxious and I joined her out of a perverse sense of interest in what she could possibly say.

"Good afternoon, sir," said Bethan brightly, smiling warmly at the man but hitching her fingers through her belt to show off the cuffs, radio, truncheon, and numerous black leather pouches. I had to admit she looked sexy as sexy can be, and if I was a single man and a decade younger I'd be smitten. I then realised that I was single, which still felt weird to admit, but I was not, and never would be, a decade younger.

"Um, hi. Is there anything wrong, officer?" The man brushed a soggy lump of hair from his eyes and glanced at me.

"No problem, sir. I'm just doing a routine check and was wondering if you would care to explain why you are here?"

The man frowned, then offered up, "Camping? This is a campsite, and I just paid the owner, a rather strange man, for a few nights. That's okay, isn't it?"

"Yes, of course, sir. May I ask what kind of tent you have?"

I saw where she was going with this now, and she'd piqued my interest.

"Ah, well, here's the funny thing," he said, eyes darting between us. "This was a spur-of-the-moment trip. I just needed to get away, so I don't actually have a tent yet. In fact, I don't even have a sleeping bag. I'm strictly a stay-at-home man usually, but something called me to the wilds of the north and with the weather promising to be so nice, I figured why not?"

"That's rather unconventional, sir," said Bethan with a frown as she placed her hands on the door as though she could halt the car if he made a break for it.

"Not really. I've been meaning to buy a tent for years, so figured if I made the trip, I'd be forced to get one finally."

"Where'd you come from?" I asked. "Have far to drive?"

"No, not far," he snapped, frowning. "Who are you? Why all these questions?"

"I'm just another camper helping out Constable Jones here," I said brightly, my suspicions about this man deepening.

"What's your name, please?" asked Bethan formally.

"Barry. Barry Simms."

"You don't look like a Barry," I blurted, and I couldn't understand why.

Bethan frowned at me, then turned back to Barry. "So, just to be clear, sir," she said rather loudly to get his attention, "you've come camping but you don't have a tent or a sleeping bag, and I'm guessing no other supplies either? Not even a torch?" Bethan leaned in through the window to take a look and I tried my best to do the same. She smelled nice.

"I have a torch, and food. Although, I did eat the food. Driving makes you hungry," he said, smiling but looking uncomfortable.

He reached into the glovebox after opening it, rummaged around, and pulled out a very powerful, and quite professional torch. There was also a phone, a camera, numerous scrunched-up pieces of paper, and several packs of boiled sweets.

"I see," said Bethan, squinting.

Was she trying to intimidate the man?

"Nice camera," I said.

He glanced at the open glovebox then snapped it shut. "Thanks. I'm a keen birdwatcher. This is a great spot."

"Oh, what are your favourite gulls?" I asked innocently.

"Um, terns. I love a tern. Now, if that's all?"

"Yes, that will be all, sir. But please ensure you get yourself a tent soon. It gets cold at night up here on the bluff, and you certainly need a sleeping bag."

"I will, officer. Thank you. If the worst comes to the worst, I can always sleep in the car." He wound the window up, utterly unnecessary as it was beyond warm and he only had to drive across the field to park.

As he drove off, I caught sight of blankets on the back seat and piles of clothes strewn over the place. It was like he'd said. The guy had just thrown everything in hastily and come on a trip without any kind of preparation. Who does that?

We watched Barry drive to the far end of the field then park his car. He got out and glanced back at us, then turned away and stared out to sea.

"That was weird," I said.

"Trust me, you get all sorts coming to these places. Some people expect the site owners to pitch their tents for them and bring them water over. I've been called to sites because the tourists are incensed they have to do their own dishes and there's no dishwasher. Some people expect camping to be like being at home but with better views and without the housework."

"You think he had something to do with the murder?"

"No, I think he's had a fight with his wife and buggered off for a few days," said Bethan dismissively, then marched off towards the woods.

Anxious and I exchanged a confused glance then rushed to catch her up. He didn't seem like he had a wife to me. More a... I had no idea what he seemed like. A murderer maybe? What did murderers look like? Shifty, eyes too close together. Lank hair. Nervous, and jittery.

He fit the bill. But then, I probably did too.

Chapter 5

"Well?" I asked, turning away from the accusing dead eyes for the third time now.

"He's definitely dead," gulped Bethan as she giggled nervously and glanced at me.

"Sure is. Any idea who he is?"

"Nope. He's not local, or I'd recognise him. Gosh, he's really dead."

"Have you seen a dead body before?"

"Just Nana. But she was dressed up nice and in a fancy casket. This is different. Why's he such a funny colour?"

I shrugged. "I guess weird things happen when you die. Blood pooling, that kind of thing."

"Yes, right. Well, I suppose the coroner will order an autopsy and the detectives will be along soon enough. Thank you for showing me."

"You're welcome. You okay?"

"Yes, we're trained for these kinds of things, but when it's on your own patch it just seems different. More real."

"I understand. A bit different to chasing sheep," I joked, although it felt instantly wrong to do so.

Bethan whirled on me, genuinely angry. "Don't you make fun of me. I've had that my whole life. People think I'm a joke for wanting to be a police officer. It's no laughing matter. You think I like being laughed at?"

"No, of course not. Sorry, I didn't mean to be rude."

"I know. I'm sorry too. I shouldn't take it out on you. And I'm not being very professional. I should secure the scene. Yes, I better do that. My boss will have my hide otherwise. Sorry to get you involved. You just wanted a relaxing holiday."

"Actually, I'm not on holiday. I live in my camper. Well, I will be. This is my first night away."

"You don't have a home?"

"Yes, the VW. Time for a new start. A new life. I messed up the old one, so I'm trying again."

"Sounds lovely. But won't you miss home?"

"No, not home. Just my wife."

"You left her behind? That's... weird."

"We're divorced. It's a long story. Now, the crime scene tape. Can I help?"

Bethan nodded, so we set up the cordon around the body. I showed her where I'd found the man in the lane, and she studied the spot carefully, marked the area, but left the access open.

I milled about while Bethan checked either side of the road, presumably looking for clues, but she found nothing. With little else to do, we wrapped the body back up, mindful of disturbing the poor guy, then headed back to the campsite. Bethan thanked me for the help and said that her superiors would most likely want to talk with me, and not to leave; she was going to talk with Dai about who'd been staying, who'd left, and who on earth the man was. I got the impression Dai didn't keep that close an eye on things, no matter what he'd said, but he might have a record if the guy had booked online.

Walking back to the campervan felt like an anti-climax after such a busy start to the trip, but Anxious ran around happily sniffing the hedgerows, tail going fast as he tracked rabbits and zig-zagged this way and that.

Feeling like I should do something, but not knowing what, and with time getting on if I wanted to make my dinner, I put the terrible incident to the back of my mind and focused on prepping the ingredients. With the pot on to heat, I added the bacon, the sizzle music to my ears. When it was done, I removed the bacon and a generous knob of butter was added. I let it melt, then dropped in the onions, and let them sauté, before adding the garlic and vegetables. Once golden, I browned the meat, the sizzling of the pork music to my ears. As the pork darkened, I added in the beef and sausage and kept an eye on it so nothing burned. Happy with how it was progressing, I continued preparing the rest of the one-pot meal and after the stock was added I let it come to a slow boil then turned the heat right down, put the lid on, and left it to work its magic.

The smell inside was divine, and even outside the heady aromas were a delight. Anxious sat directly outside the door, eyes on the pot, willing it with his incredible sense of righteous deserving of all things meaty for it to hurry up and cook as he wanted his dinner.

"It'll be hours yet," I laughed. "We need a distraction while it cooks, or we'll be driven mad. How about a walk?"

At the mention of the W word, Anxious' ears pricked up, his tail swept the grass, and his eyes locked on mine, boring into my very soul as his excitement built. Never mind that he was off the lead in an open field, the mention of a walk still excited him no end.

A stroll along the beach was tempting, but I thought it best to be able to keep an eye on the pot. Last thing I wanted were any accidents on my first day. Burning down the campervan definitely fit into that category. Instead, I decided a wander around the campsite would be safer, and we could go for our main excursion after dinner. Wandering along the beach at sunset held a romantic appeal, even if it was just the two of us.

"Let's start here and work our way around," I suggested.

Anxious was keen, so we set off down the gentle rise. I waved to a couple sitting in their chairs outside their tent, both tanned and happy, a folding table with a bottle of wine half drunk while they enjoyed the warm evening.

Next, I passed a lone camper smoking what definitely didn't smell like tobacco, but he smiled warmly and even extended the joint. It wasn't my thing, so I shook my head, smiled, and carried on. Around the perimeter, I passed other groups or single campers in a mix of tiny one-man tents for hikers, or huge family tents with all the bells and whistles. Some people took their camping very seriously. With awnings, gazebos, wind breaks, and fire bowls. But when you noted the families chatting happily, making dinner and drinking wine while the children ran around playing, you had to appreciate the effort they'd made.

Several youngsters came up to us to say hello to Anxious, who behaved himself impeccably and let the children pat him. I passed the spot where Barry Sims had parked his Volvo, but I'd already watched him leave, presumably to source a tent. He'd left behind a pile of clothes spilling out of a cardboard box of all things, presumably to mark his pitch, but it seemed weird and as I passed, something clicked in my head. There was more than one type of tern, wasn't there? He said he was an avid birdwatcher, so should know that. I was sure there were Arctic Terns, Common, and weren't there Black Terns too? I vaguely recalled a documentary Min had forced me to watch, as she loved anything to do with nature. What was Barry's game?

At the bottom of the hill, a large hedge and stock-proof fencing ensured neither the animals nor the guests threw themselves off the cliff. It afforded excellent protection from the wind that no doubt raged at certain times of the year, but if you stepped back a little you still got a magnificent view of the sea.

Several lone campers had hunkered down here for the protection. Most tents were unoccupied, the inhabitants presumably off hiking or taking in the beach. As we approached the far end, Anxious and I paused at a commotion. Two men wearing smart dark clothes were shouting at each other angrily; both had shaved heads and were almost identical. A smaller man emerged from the large tent and glanced around then marched forward and beckoned them both with a crook of his finger.

The men ceased their shouting and stomped over like naughty children. They stopped in front of the one in charge, who brushed a hand through wavy sandy hair then spoke too softly for me to hear. With Anxious as an excuse as he rushed ahead to sniff out rabbits, I strode forward casually and called out to him halfheartedly, hoping for a change that he'd ignore me. With his body half buried in the hedge, I got my wish and smiled as I waved to the three men now watching me.

"Hi, sorry about the dog. He's got the scent of rabbits. He's a Terrier, and you know what they're like."

"What are they like?" asked one of the beefy men. The other two moved beside him and watched us with cold eyes, none of them smiling.

"They like to hunt. They love to chase things. Anxious is a good boy, though, aren't you, Anxious?" I called loudly. He backed out from the hedge, shook himself out, then rushed over and sat by my side, head cocked as he watched the men. A low growl emerged from deep within his chest and his hackles rose. He didn't trust them. "Be nice, Anxious. These men are just enjoying their holiday."

"He's called Anxious?" asked the smart man, brushing a blade of grass from his tailored yellow shirt and scowling at the hint of nature.

"Yes, long story, but he's not."

"Not what?" asked the other big guy with a frown of confusion.

"Anxious."

"You just said he was," he accused, pointing a meaty finger at me.

"It's his name, not his current emotional state," I explained.

The weasel-like man chuckled and slapped both men on the back. "I like this guy. He's funny."

"He is?" asked the other.

"Yeah, he is."

"So, you fellas having a fun holiday? Been anywhere nice? Are you from Liverpool? Is that your accent? I guess it's not too far from here. Lots of Liverpudlians come to North Wales to holiday, don't they?"

"You ask a lot of questions," growled beefcake number one.

"Hey, relax. This guy is just being friendly. That's how it is on campsites," scolded the one who somehow was clearly in charge. He turned to me, smiling, and said, "Yes, we're from Liverpool. Just a short trip to get some sea air. A bonding experience," he laughed, turning to the others. "Am I right, guys?"

"Yeah, course. Good to get away from the missus for a while."

Beefcake number two nodded vehemently. "That's right. Works do. Boys' weekend kind of thing."

"Well, enjoy. It's a lovely spot," I said, then called Anxious and waved as we headed back up the hill.

"See you around," said the slender boss, eyes intent.

"Sure."

Once halfway up the hill, I turned to watch the two bodyguards—that's what they seemed like—glance my way before they were ushered into the privacy of the seemingly brand new tent by their leader.

"That was odd. Anxious, what do you make of that?"

Anxious growled as he looked back at them.

"That's what I thought. They seem suspicious to me. Maybe we should tell Bethan?" As we continued our walk, I considered what to do. The police would question everyone on the site, no doubt, and could make their own conclusions. I'd just be interfering. And besides, surely the killer would be long gone, not hanging around and risking getting caught? Best to leave this well alone. It wasn't my business, and I certainly wasn't better equipped than the police to figure this out.

After we completed our circuit of the campsite, both of us buoyed by the friendliness of almost everyone, but with nobody else seeming suspicious, we returned to the VW and the unmistakable aromas of a one-pot masterpiece.

I checked on the pot, pleased to find the stove had worked flawlessly, although I kicked myself for making such an amateur move and leaving it unattended. I needed to make a list of do's and don'ts, as I assumed this was a definite no-no.

Nevertheless, it smelled divine, and with Anxious getting rather, er, anxious, and my energy levels flagging after what had been a more interesting day than anticipated, I readied a bowl and cutlery, along with Anxious' dog bowl, and willed the stew to finish.

A distraction soon came in the form of the police. A veritable squadron descended on the campsite, with constables, plain-clothes detectives, and some higher-ups judging by the way everyone chased around after them, gathering at the farmhouse then dispersing. I guessed there were already a number of them at the crime scene, assuming it actually was the crime scene, which I doubted, whilst the officers began to question everyone, oblivious until now about what had happened.

Bethan was with two detectives, but halfway across the field they stopped and she pointed. They had words before she turned and stormed off, clearly unhappy about being left out of the loop.

The two detectives made straight for me, so I asked Anxious to behave and when they arrived the little guy was the epitome of an obedient dog, smiling and wagging and generally doing whatever he could to ensure they didn't arrest him for crimes against the local rabbit population.

The male detective was very nondescript, with one of those faces you'd be hard-pushed to recall, with average hair, average brown eyes, average height, average everything. Even his clothes were so plain that I couldn't keep a picture of him in my mind even with him in front of me.

The woman, on the other hand, was utterly memorable. Her tan was a weird orange colour, most likely from a bottle, and she was larger than life in every way. Wide of girth, short of stature, tattoos on her arms, and wearing a bright balloon of a dress of a Caribbean style, with a shock of bleached blond hair in need of a touch-up.

"Mr. Max Effort?" she asked, consulting a notebook she pulled out of the folds of her flapping dress. "Is that correct?"

"Yes," I sighed. "It's correct."

"Hey, no judgement from us," she sniggered. "Do you hate your parents?"

"Yes, very much. If I could get away with it, I'd murder them in their beds and scratch my damn name into their foreheads. With a blunt pencil."

A frosty silence descended as the two upholders of the law gawped at me. Heat rose from my chest to my neck and I shook my head at my utter idiocy before adding, "Sorry, that was a lame joke under any circumstance, but now especially. I know it doesn't seem like it, but I'm not a homicidal, parent-murdering maniac. Promise."

"Well, that's alright then," she beamed, her booming voice echoing around the campsite. "Although," she confided with a wink, "I'd be temped."

"Julia, can we get on?" sighed the man, looking bored.

"Yeah, sure. Take a chill pill, Malc."

"It's Malcolm. How many times do I have to tell you?"

"As many as you want, I'll still call you Malc." Julia turned her attention back to me and after making proper introductions, asked if I could explain what I'd seen, and what had happened, so I went through everything with her the same as I had with Bethan.

Five minutes later, Malc said, "Thank you, sir. If you think of anything else, please get in touch."

"That's it?" I asked, surprised.

"Unless there's something you haven't told us?" asked Julia.

"Um, no. I just assumed you'd want a written statement and to ask more questions."

"We have your name and contact number, but if you no longer have a home address it does make things more awkward," she admitted. "But I trust you, and you seem like a nice guy, so if you say you're hanging around for a few days that's good enough for us. Don't bail on us, so if we think of any follow-up questions we can find you. Deal?"

"Yes, sure. What do you think happened?"

"Someone killed the poor guy and wrapped him in a tent," said Malc like it was utterly obvious. Which it was.

"I mean, why dump him there? Why kill him at all? And where are his clothes?"

"His clothes most likely had evidence on them so were removed. As to why he was killed, or why he was left in the road, that's police business and none of yours," said Malc, voice monotone.

"Then have a good day," I snapped, annoyed by his attitude.

"Hey, Max, no need for that," warned Julia. "Malc here is just a grump—"

"I am not!"

"—so ignore him. You've been very helpful. We need to get on and speak to everyone else. See you around." With a cheery wave, Julia turned and left.

Malc nodded to me then joined her.

"Weird," I muttered once they'd made their way down the field.

Anxious barked his agreement, then dashed over to the campervan and sat outside, tail wagging, casting pleading glances my way then locking eyes on the bubbling pot.

"Yes, it's definitely time for dinner. You want to help dish up?" I laughed.

Anxious leaped into the van and spun in a circle so I joined him and with an oven glove lifted the lid. The van filled with steam that billowed out of the open doors, sending Anxious into a frenzy of drool and spinning. It smelled as amazing as I'd expected, and the joy it brought me was indescribable.

For years, I'd dreamed of having the time to do such things, but my life was hectic, bordering on insanity, with no time for anything apart from work. Looking back on it, I lamented how utterly foolish I'd been when life was about so much more. All the things I'd missed out on, the fun I'd foregone, just to chase some exalted position that never brought happiness, just additional stress and more work. But it was an excuse. I'd chosen the way I pursued my career, picked the hours, and inflicted it on myself. Plenty of top chefs managed work and home life just fine. I had not been one of them.

I'd lost my wife, and given her our home even though it was little recompense, and yet at least I'd learned my lesson before I'd died of a heart attack. So, it may have been a simple pot of food, but it held tremendous significance for me, and this truly felt like the beginning of the rest of my life.

With a generous portion of pork, beef, and sausage for both of us, then Anxious' chickpeas mushed up so he wouldn't know they were there as he wasn't keen, I took both bowls outside and placed his down then sat in my chair and we tucked in.

It. Was. Amazing.

Chapter 6

"Ugh, where am I supposed to put everything?" I complained to Anxious who was sitting on the bench seat watching my every move just in case there happened to be more delicious stew. There wasn't. We'd eaten three bowls each and he'd even licked the pot clean. Not exactly hygienic, but I figured it would give me a start on the, thankfully, minimal washing up.

Then things got a little awkward.

Used to either commercial sinks—not that I ever had to do the dishes as I was too fancy for that—or sinks at home that consisted of the main bowl, a smaller secondary one, then a large drainer, I was struggling with the concept of washing a very large, and extremely heavy, cast-iron pot in a sink smaller than the pot. After waiting an inordinate amount of time for a kettle full of water to boil, I'd decided the best bet was to simply wash the beast outside. So far, so good.

With the wrist-wrenching pot finally clean, I turned my attention to the bowls and cutlery and whatnot from the evening's feast that sat soaking in the sink. Things unravelled quickly. I washed my bowl then didn't know where to put it. Next to it was the compact hob, and the other side wasn't much use either. I resorted to placing the chopping board over the thankfully cold hob and resting a tea towel on it then putting the bowls, cups, and cutlery there. But it soaked through, and ran onto the hob and down the cupboards, so I was left with soapy water streaks and puddles everywhere.

"How do people do this for a family or when they use lots of pots and pans?" I asked Anxious, who had given up by now and was curled up and snoring on the bench seat. Turning back to the mess, I realised I now had a bowl that was very full of dirty water. "I didn't think this through at all," I grumbled, then decided to clear everything else away before tackling this problem.

Once I'd dried up, cleaned up, and moaned up, I didn't know what to do with the water in the sink. Should I just pull out the plug? Where did it go? What had the guy said when I'd bought it? Ah yes, there were two containers under the sink. One for fresh water for the tap, the other to collect grey water. The clean water had a spout outside to fill it up for convenience, a modification done by the original owner, but the grey waste needed to be emptied manually.

On hands and knees, I reached up and pulled the plug nervously, then ducked back down rapidly to check it wasn't going to pour over the entire van. It was beyond satisfying to watch the dirty water gush into the collection vessel. Note to self: remember to empty it in a day or two, and fill up with fresh water.

There were a thousand little things like this that I encountered, along with worrying about gas levels, how did the fridge even work on gas, how long would my power last, and on the list went. I knew it was early days and everything would slot into place over time, but it wasn't the relaxing first day I'd envisaged where I'd be lazing around and enjoying the scenery.

After a thorough wipe-down of the sink, tap, and chopping board because old habits die hard and I knew the importance of cleanliness even if I did want to get a few more germs into my system, I sighed with relief and finally sat down to chill out in my chair. It was an expensive model with an angled back, a cup holder, and a foot rest, so I kicked off my Crocs—the best for campsite living as they slipped on and off easily—and put my feet up.

After baking in Vee—I'd decided that would be my name for her—it was sheer delight to feel the breeze coming in off the sea. It remained incredibly hot, but not unbearably so, and stripped down to my shorts I felt truly content and relaxed. This was what it was all about. New experiences, new struggles, new adventures, but with the weather for company rather than angry faces and shouting chefs.

If Min was here it would have been perfect, but I had to get that out of my mind. This was a new start, and I surprised myself with just how much I was enjoying it. Anxious came to join me and curled up at my feet, his belly looking decidedly tight against the skin. We'd both have to watch it, or we'd be obese in a few months.

I watched the other campers come and go, trying to get back to enjoying themselves after their fun being interrupted by the police and the inevitable questions. For a while, the campsite was rife with gossip and concern as people discussed the fact someone had been found dead, but from what I overheard the police hadn't told anyone it was actually a murder. I guessed they weren't allowed to discuss such things, especially before a thorough investigation and they had time to track the next of kin. If they ever found out who he was.

Things began to settle down as more pressing matters came to the fore. Namely, enjoying a short break. Soon the campsite was again awash with the sounds of people laughing and joking, kicking balls around with the kids, or sitting outside their tents enjoying an evening tipple while they gossiped about the evening's excitement.

My eyes drifted to Barry Simms, the strange fellow who had arrived without a tent. It was quite the show. He must have arrived back while I was cleaning up, as he was now struggling with a compact tent, scratching his head and repeatedly checking the instructions as he attempted to put it up.

This was the other fun thing about camping. Watching people be as crap as you. If you've never seen a flustered couple try to put a pop-up tent back into a bag then you have yet to know what real comedy is. Barry was clearly not a man of the wilds. He inserted the tent pole sections together like they were foreign objects liable to attack at any moment, and once he slotted them into place and tried to run them through the tent and pin them into the pegs it became a true comedy of errors. He'd clearly put the wrong pole through the wrong colour-coded loops so it simply wouldn't fit. In a huff, he tried to yank it out, but of course the poles separated, and he was tugging them so hard he was liable to rip the cord threaded through them.

I knew better than to offer my assistance. And there was something odd about the guy. He was up to something, but what that could be I couldn't fathom. Finally, he managed to get everything together, then banged in the pegs and did a half-hearted job with the guy ropes. He stood, nodded with satisfaction, and marched over to the boot of his Volvo, tripped over a rope, smacked his head on the bumper, and fell in a heap. I was ready to chase down to help him, but he sprang upright, jumped around to check if anyone saw so I lowered my head and closed my eyes, trying my best to stifle a laugh, then peeked a moment later to see him fighting with a sleeping bag and winning a small victory as it popped out of the tiny bag it came in.

The smells of barbecue and the shouts of happy children lulled me into a half sleep, but it was only just gone half seven and way too early for bed, so I decided to take Anxious on a proper walk. We'd hit the beach tomorrow for a morning stroll, but I didn't fancy driving again today and wondered what'd happened to the body by the road, so decided to just walk up one of the dedicated footpaths that skirted the campsite and see where it took us.

I grabbed his lead, pocketed the poo bags, and changed into more sensible footwear then slipped a T-shirt on.

"You set?" I asked the cute little guy as he sat waiting impatiently. The moment I'd begun to get ready he was on the case, sure something exciting was about to happen.

Anxious barked his status, that of always keen, so I told him to stay close and off we went. I steered clear of the police officers by the farmhouse still questioning people as they arrived back at the site for the evening, and wondered how long they would stay and if they already had any suspects. Anxious remained by my side as we went through a gate onto a path. It was a steep climb but well worn, and after several minutes the dense undergrowth of ferns and bracken gave way to rolling countryside where sheep grazed contentedly.

"Do not chase those sheep," I warned. "Or you'll have to go on the lead."

Anxious glanced at the big balls of wool then back at me, as if asking why on earth he would want to do such a thing. I laughed at his angled head, then said, "Okay, off you go then. But come back when I call."

He was off like a rocket, sniffing the tiny trails invisible to the human eye but lit up like a runway to a dog intent on tracking anything smaller than he was. Anxious had spent most of his life off lead. He was easy to train, never made a mess in the house even as a puppy once he got over his initial burst of crazy, and had never shown an interest in chasing anything larger than a rabbit. He adored chasing the taunting squirrels, too, but unlike many Terriers he would never try to actually kill them. He lived for the tracking, and was content to eat only what I gave him.

He often accompanied me to work, although he always had to stay out of the kitchen much to his disgust, so we bonded more than he and Min did. He loved her, and it was very tough for her to relinquish him to me, but we all knew it was for the best. He had spent his entire life by my side, and I couldn't imagine a day without him. We'd always worked together, rested together, and slept together, so I thanked my lucky stars Min was kind enough to not try to take him from me. I really would have been a lost soul without my best buddy.

At the top of this section of hill were a series of rocks perfect for resting, so I settled down and slowly caught my breath. The views were astonishing, with the cliffs to the west and the curve of the land to the east going up into England. But it was the sight of the sea and the beaches far below that were truly beautiful. It made me question how such magnificence could possibly have come about.

Feeling recovered, I continued the climb, passing several abandoned stone buildings little more than rubble, several squat shepherd's shelters that seemed to still be in use and had been repaired, then we made it to the top of the next section where the path split east and west.

"Which way?" I asked Anxious.

He tore off to the west, so west it was.

Several minutes later, we came to a large farmhouse. There were no vehicles, and nobody around, but it wasn't quite derelict either. The roof was intact, rotten windows still in place, even curtains, but the glass was filthy and the front door was ajar. I guess it had just been abandoned years ago, probably because it was an exposed site.

It was built partially into the hillside and from the rear you could walk onto the long, shallow sloping roof. I'd noticed that many buildings were like this with the front half of the houses shorter with a steep pitch, the back lower and at a gentle angle. I assumed it was so the prevailing wind was lessened, but surely the wind would come from the sea, not from behind us?

As a sudden gust picked up, I realised my mistake as I was nearly bowled over. Yep, they knew what they were doing alright.

A low wall, fallen in places, circled the property, with several ruined barns and animal shelters built into it. Everything was covered in weeds and grass, with ferns and moss nestled in the damp crevices, making it feel very romantic and intimate even though the place was eerily quiet.

Back around the front, I pushed on the door gently and peered inside. It was dark and smelled musty, but I spied furniture and even rugs on the worn black flagstones. Did someone live here?

Chapter 7

"Max?" came a familiar voice as the pressure eased from my ankle.

I spun my sore backside until I was facing the mystery intruder and almost collapsed with relief as I realised who the "killer" was. "Bethan? What are you doing here? You scared me half to death. Um, you aren't a secret homicidal maniac, I don't suppose?"

"No, I am not! And I thought I'd captured the killer," she laughed nervously, brushing her hair from her eyes and smiling. "Um, you aren't the killer, are you? You could have been trying to bluff me then." Her eyes darted to the door where Anxious had turned to make his way back to us. He licked my cheek, then bounded into Bethan's lap and with his tail going a mile a minute he placed his paws on her shoulders and began to lick her chin like it was covered in peanut butter.

"No, and promise you aren't?" I chuckled, watching her squirm.

"Definitely not. Anxious, what are you doing? Stop licking me," she squealed with delight.

Anxious, his work done, happiness expressed, jumped down and sat, clearly waiting for the next fun game to begin.

"Thanks for being such an excellent guard dog, Anxious," I said, mock serious.

He wagged happily, checked nothing else was about to happen, then wandered off outside.

"Are you okay?" I asked Bethan, getting to my feet then reaching out to haul her up.

She took my hand and I helped her stand then she said, "Fine, thanks. You gave me quite a scare. I really thought I was going to catch the killer. What are you doing here?" Bethan scowled at the state of her uniform, so brushed herself down as best she could.

I realised I was just as dusty, so slapped at my shorts, noting my knees were grazed with light scratches, and soon we were coughing in a cloud of dust so I indicated the kitchen and we moved to the relatively clean air.

"I was walking and found this cottage, so was just being nosy. It's a cool place."

"Used to be lived in until only ten years ago, if you can believe that. Old Mrs. Jones, and no, she wasn't a relation, was born in this house. She died here too. Right in front of the fire. She never had electricity, refused to have it installed, the water is from a stream, and she lived here her entire life."

"Wow, that's hardcore. That must have been a tough existence."

"It was, but she lived until she was ninety-eight so she must have been doing something right. No processed food, no technology, not even a TV. She had a radio. That was it for entertainment."

"Sounds idyllic but boring at the same time." I couldn't imagine such a life, but wasn't I striving for a modern version of that? Maybe not as extreme, but I was certainly coming to realise there was more to life than our current generation had been led to believe was important.

"She was hard as nails and the grumpiest woman you're ever likely to meet. She used to chase us kids with a stick when we came up here to play."

"Not a sweet old lady then?"

"No, she was vicious," grinned Bethan, eyes losing focus as she reminisced about being a young lass. "She never had a nice word for anyone, and even though everyone around here did all they could to help her, fetching food, sorting out any paperwork for her, all the modern things she didn't know how to do, she never said thank you. She couldn't read very well, or write, but in her own way she was a gentle soul. She just wanted to be left alone to do her own thing. Some people said she was a witch."

"You kids made up stories about her, eh?"

"Not just us kids. Adults too. There was something about her. I wasn't going to come, but I've been thinking about this case and figured I should check the abandoned cottages around here, just to be sure."

"Sounds like a good idea. So, no leads then? What did the detectives say?"

"They..." Bethan frowned, then confided, "I shouldn't really be telling you anything. We're not supposed to. But they're out of ideas. We're going through any missing persons reports which will take a while, but there should be news this evening. So far nobody has been reported missing, so the next step is to question the campsite owners to see if anyone booked in or out matching the description. The detectives or doing that now. I was told to go home for the evening as nobody at the campsite knew anything or seemed suspicious, even though I didn't like the look of the guys down in the corner of the field. There really aren't many places to check around here apart from a couple of sites and the large static home communities down by the sea, but I'm sure something will turn up."

"They didn't want you to go and ask around?"

"Nope, they dismissed me like they always do. I'm new to the force, and they don't think I'm up to it yet. It's so unfair. I'm better than most of those lazy officers. I work hard, but they just won't let me in. It's because I'm young, and a girl."

"And pretty," I said.

Bethan blushed, then asked, "You think so?"

"Sure. You're very pretty. Don't get any ideas though. I'm old enough to be your dad."

"In your dreams," she laughed, her face brightening at the compliment. "I think the real reason's because they see me as some dumb country bumpkin. Quite a few of the officers in Rhyl are from Liverpool, so they have city experience. Others come from larger towns in the area. It's not a huge police force, but a lot of them are old-timers as people aren't exactly queueing up to join. They don't trust us new recruits. I'm only a year in, so..." Bethan shrugged.

"I'm sure you're a real asset, and you'll prove yourself. This why you're snooping around when you should be at home with your feet up watching the TV?"

"If I go home, it's to my parents either bickering or watching some rubbish reality show. Not my idea of fun. So I figured I'd check a few things out. This is between us, okay? I'll be in real trouble if my boss thinks I've been blabbing about a case to a member of the public."

"Mum's the word." I zipped my mouth shut and threw away the key.

"Thanks."

"So, any clues? What do you think happened?" I asked, keen despite the fright I'd received.

"No clues. Nobody knows. It's a real head-scratcher. I hung around when the coroner's team arrived, and I watched the detectives too. They inspected the body and there was no sign of any wounds that could have killed him."

"That's what I thought too! I saw the blood, but there weren't any cuts I could see. Nothing on the back of the poor guy's head?"

"He did have a nasty gash there. There were an awful lot of bruises too. More on the back than the front. My guess is the blood pooled because of the tent, and you probably made it go everywhere by rolling him about."

"Or it was someone else's blood. There might be more than one victim."

"Who knows?" shrugged Bethan. "It's got me and some of the other officers a bit freaked out, actually. We roam around the area at all hours, and there's never been anything like this before."

"Maybe you shouldn't be wandering around derelict cottages in the evening on your own then."

"Maybe you shouldn't," she scolded. "Don't forget, I may be younger than you, but I'm trained. I know how to use my truncheon, was top of my class at self-defence, and I've got a radio."

"Fair point," I conceded. "Maybe we should get going?"

"Yes, I think that's best. Promise you won't mention our chat to anyone?"

"Of course not. I promise. It's not like you're giving me all the secrets anyway."

"No, but I'd still be in trouble. We aren't meant to discuss open investigations with anyone."

We moved to the front door, then I slapped my forehead and said, "I forgot! The fireplace."

"What about it?"

I showed Bethan the inglenook, and the smouldering wood, and she took her time studying the embers, even going so far as to shine her torch up the chimney.

"Oh my!" she gasped.

"What is it? A clue?"

"Come and hold the torch. I can't reach."

I ducked back into the inglenook, then took the offered torch and shone it up the sooty chimney. "You smell nice," I blurted, unable to help myself. We were pressed against each other, and I couldn't help taking a cheeky sniff, even though as I said it I knew it was weird.

Bethan stiffened.

"Sorry, that was ultra-weird, right?"

"Very."

"Damn, I don't know what's wrong with me. I honestly am not trying anything funny. You're sweet and all, but way too young."

"Sweet? Sweet! I'm a police officer. I don't want to be sweet. I want to be mean."

"I meant sweet in a very tough and scary way, obviously," I laughed.

"Gee, thanks! Now hold that torch steady. Shine it there where I'm pointing."

I angled the torch until the light fixed on something wedged high up in the chimney. Bethan stood on tiptoe then grabbed it and yanked down with a grunt.

Soot and the object crashed down into the fireplace, erupting in a thick fog that sent us coughing our way out of the cramped space.

"Your face is filthy," I laughed.

"So is yours. You look like a panda."

We smiled at each other as we wiped away the soot from our eyes, then locked them on the black object still in the fireplace. With a whoosh, the embers caught the fine particles and the object itself and it began to burn.

Bethan raced forward, snatched it up, then dropped it on the floor and stomped out the flames. With a gasp, she stepped back and we stared down at the dark bundle.

"What is it?" I asked.

"Clothes, I think." We squinted at the bundle through gritty eyes, but it was hard to make out much.

I returned to the fireplace and retrieved a stick leaning against the wall, the end burned where it had been used to poke the fire.

"Here, use this. You better do it as you know what you're doing."

"Thanks." Bethan took the stick then carefully untangled the ball of what appeared to be nothing but rags. She worked slowly and methodically, never touching them directly, until the whole thing had been unravelled. She wiped the sheen of sweat from her brow and tucked her hair behind her ears as we stood and looked down on our find.

"A boiler suit? A grey boiler suit. Why would it be stuffed up the chimney? Is there a logo? I can't see one."

"Let me see." Bethan bent again and rubbed at the sooty stains over the breast of the button-down workwear, revealing a blue patch logo. "It's the local electrical company, e-energy. They've been changing over a lot of rural properties to smart meters so people can monitor their usage."

"We had one of those."

"We?"

"Me and my wife. We're divorced now. Did I say?"

"Yes, and I'm sorry to hear that. So, you're having a mid-life crisis and thought hitting the road would solve all your problems?"

"Not quite, and I'd never thought about it like that. Maybe I am," I chuckled, not sure if that was good or bad. "But I'm not middle-aged," I said.

"Course not," she laughed.

"So, what does this mean? The work outfit of someone employed by this electric company? Do they do regular work too?"

"Yeah, sure. They're the main name around here now. They cover a lot of the county, actually, and get subcontracted to install the meters. Even Grandad has one, although he says he doesn't trust it and wished he'd never had it as now he's paranoid about boiling the kettle. He reckons his bills skyrocketed after it was installed, and is always complaining. He almost has a heart attack every time he has to run the lights when it's lambing time. The heat lamps for the little poorly ones make his head hurt when he sees how much it costs."

"The prices sure have gone up rapidly lately. It's double what it was a few years ago," I agreed.

"But this is a clue!" said Bethan, beaming. "Maybe this belonged to the victim? Maybe he worked for e-energy? That's the name, see?"

I bent to join her and once she disturbed more of the soot and blew on the logo it was easy enough to make out. A modern lowercase design with "e-energy" in digital looking script with a light bulb clearly shaped into the first letter e.

"We found our first clue!" I shouted, then clamped my hand over my mouth. I looked around warily, suddenly aware that if there had been someone here either today or yesterday they might have returned or already be hiding. "We should leave. What if the killer's waiting for us outside? They might be back to collect the evidence."

Bethan's good mood turned serious and she glanced around the room then nodded. "You're right. Let's be quiet, and let's go. Right now." She pulled out a white plastic bag from a leather pouch on her utility belt and used the stick to put the uniform inside then sealed it up.

"Is this a crime scene now?" I asked.

"I guess it is. I'm going to have to call this in. You should go. I'll explain what happened, but I'm sorry to say that the detectives will want to ask you more questions."

"I'll wait here. If I go back to the campsite, they'll be around when others are trying to sleep, and we don't want them to disturb everyone. Plus, people will worry. They're already jittery enough after earlier. You call it in, we'll make sure we're alone, then I'll post Anxious on guard duty. Come to think of it, where is he?"

He'd been gone a while and hadn't even returned after hearing the shouting and excitement. Normally, the first sign of anyone having fun and he'd come running, yapping his readiness to play.

"Good idea, and I guess it does make sense for you to wait here."

We went outside and Bethan walked off a ways to get a better signal on her radio then reported what we'd found. When she returned, she said that the detectives would be out as soon as possible but it might take them a while.

I nodded, more concerned about Anxious, but I wasn't sure if I should call for him or remain quiet and search for the little guy. Bethan and I both studied the surrounding countryside. Because the stone wall circled the property, there were plenty of outcroppings for people to hide behind as well as the trees that protected the cottage from the worst of the wind, so we really were like sitting ducks here if anyone decided to try something untoward.

"I am a police officer. I am strong, capable, and not afraid. I will not be scared. I will not be scared." Bethan repeated the mantra several times then squared her shoulders, locked eyes with me, and said, "Sir, I will protect you," before nodding seriously.

"Thank you, Constable Jones. I'm glad you're here with me."

She smiled at my faith in her. I hid my grin, but in all honesty I was glad she was here. She may have been a young, fresh-faced constable, but she had a strong spirit and I didn't doubt that despite her five and a half feet, she'd give anyone what for if they tried anything on.

We heard a noise from the undergrowth and something shot out fast, heading straight for us.

"Freeze!" shouted Bethan.

I turned to find her holding her fingers out clasped in the shape of a gun, her stance wide.

"Please don't shoot my dog with your deadly digits," I pleaded, then burst out laughing.

Bethan lowered her cocked fingers, smiled awkwardly, then blew on the tips and said, "I thought it might work for a moment. Put the attacker off guard. Um, don't you dare tell anyone. I'd never live it down."

"Your loaded hands shall remain a secret," I promised, mock serious.

Bethan saw the funny side, too, and soon we were bent double with tears rolling down our cheeks. As much as anything, it had been the relief of the stress we'd both been feeling.

Suddenly, this felt very real, and very close. I was meant to be getting ready for bed, but instead I was uncovering clues that might lead to whoever killed a man and bundled him up in a tent.

Anxious sat at our feet and stared up at us, head cocked, wondering what was so funny. It was only when I wiped my eyes I realised he had something in his mouth.

"What now?" I sighed as I bent to take it from him.

With a flick of the tail, Anxious did an about turn and raced back into the bracken.

Chapter 8

"Anxious! Here, boy!" I whistled for him, but all I got was an excited bark in return. He was clearly on to something, and thought it important enough for him to remain where he was.

We stomped through the bracken, mindful of any holes, until we reached a small area surrounded by a disintegrating wall with what appeared to be a cairn in the middle. Nestled in a natural dip, the damp area was hidden from sight and would easily be overlooked unless you knew it was here. Moss grew over the wall and the soft, springy ground, shaded by stunted hawthorn and waist-high ferns.

"It's an old shepherd's sanctuary," noted Bethan. "They'd hole up here with injured animals if the weather was bad, or just come and take a snooze if it was hot. Most aren't used, but you must have seen a few on your way up."

"I did. How old are they?"

"Oh, hundreds of years. They don't make them anymore. This is one of the oldest. It's an ancient cairn, most probably to bury the dead, but for as long as anyone can remember, it's been a place for the shepherds. Imagine, once there might have been arrowheads or weapons or even gold jewellery buried with the dead, but that was long ago. We used to come and play here as kids. That's why we got into trouble with Old Mrs. Jones up at the cottage. What's he doing?"

Anxious had half his body in the low entrance to the cairn, his bum sticking up, tail wagging slowly. He growled low and menacingly then backed out, and began licking at smudges on the rocks that formed the entrance. Once happy with his work, he retrieved whatever he'd brought to us earlier, then shook it.

Satisfied he'd given it a thorough telling off, he trundled over, dropped it, then sat and looked at me expectantly.

"Good boy. Here's your treat." I gave him a biscuit so he scampered off to eat it at his leisure while Bethan and I bent to study the latest find.

"More uniform?" I suggested as Bethan turned over the scrap of almost rotten cloth with a twig.

"Looks like it. Or just someone's old clothes. Surely there can't be more boiler suits? Why would he need more than one? Okay, that was a daft question. If he's an e-energy employee then he'd have a few, I expect. What I meant was, why would another be hidden?"

"Why would the first one be hidden?" I asked.

"Good question. Let's take a look inside." Bethan removed her torch, turned it on, and we crawled forward on hands and knees into the low opening of the cairn. A huge slab of rock acted as the lintel, with a square piece of slate toppled sideways beside the entrance I assumed used to act as a door. The moment we passed under it I had to push a rising sense of panic down that the whole structure, no matter that it had stood for centuries, would choose this exact moment to collapse.

We scooted our legs around to sit, impossible to stand, and the torch flickered. Bethan slapped it into her palm and it sprang to life. She shone it around the interior, highlighting piles of wool presumably used as a makeshift bed by shepherds of the past, until she came to a sudden stop and we both screamed.

"Get out! Go, go, go!" Bethan shrieked as she shoved me through the opening and I hurried outside. I dragged her out as she kicked with her feet against the dirt in an utter panic then hauled her upright. We took several steps back, both of us panting, before I bent over with my hands on my thighs, trying to recover.

"Was that a... a... human skeleton?"

"I'm pretty sure it was. At least, part of one. My guess is animals have been in there and..."

"Eaten it?" I gasped.

"Yes, eaten it."

"What would do that?"

"Anything. Foxes, birds, rats, maybe a badger. They eat whatever they can find."

"I do not want to be eaten by a badger," I shivered.

"Neither do I.

"Half his ribs were missing, and I think those were his legs in the middle of the floor. I thought it was a dead sheep at first. It was a human, right?"

"Yes, absolutely. The body's been there a while, though, I reckon. No way could it be so... so eaten otherwise. And there's more cloth too. E-energy have some serious explaining to do."

"Remind me never to get them to fit a meter," I mumbled, trying to reconcile what I'd seen with the beauty of the landscape. It just didn't fit. Surrounded by such raw, rugged majesty when here before us lay the remains of a person.

"Bethan?"

"Yes?" she asked, turning.

"What the hell is going on here?"

"I have absolutely no idea."

Anxious began to bark incessantly, then a voice called out, "Hello?"

"Is it the killer?" I whispered.

"No, worse."

"Two of them?"

"No, even worse," sighed Bethan.

"Three?" I gasped.

"No, it's the detectives. You ready for this? It's going to be intense."

And it was.

Very.

For hours.

By the time I'd hung around waiting for Bethan to explain to the assorted detectives and bosses what on earth was going on, their eyes widening the more she told, then explained why I was here, how we came to be together, and what I'd seen, all whilst trying to ensure I didn't get her into trouble or break a promise, I was beyond exhausted.

Finally, I was told I could leave. I couldn't get out of there fast enough. Bethan was given permission to escort me to the campsite as I'd never make it without a torch anyway, so we headed down the hill with Anxious plodding along sleepily beside us. The path seemed different than on the way up. More twisty, with switchbacks, and what was breathtaking in daylight felt menacing and dangerous now, the uneven ground treacherous.

"Didn't they want you to stay?" I asked.

"No, not really. I think the detectives were put out that I found out more than them. And they aren't too happy with there being another body."

"Think they're linked?" I couldn't see her eyes, but I guessed by her intake of breath I got my answer. "Sure, that was a dumb question. Of course they are. If there was a boiler suit hidden in the chimney and probably one in the cairn, then they must be related to the guy in the tent, right?"

"It's a crazy coincidence otherwise. One day and two bodies."

"Yes, but the skeleton has been there for ages. It might not be linked to our guy."

"Maybe, but I think it is. Someone killed him and stuffed that boiler suit up the chimney."

"Why would they do that? What possible reason? Why not just dump it somewhere? Why hide it?"

"That's for the detectives to find out. I doubt they'll let me anywhere near this, even though it was us who discovered the clues."

"What will you do tomorrow?"

"Make my report, see what I can uncover, and most likely get assigned some boring patrol duty, or maybe if I'm lucky get to visit the other campsites and ask questions."

"That would be good, right? You might discover something."

"Max, you're a nice guy, if a little weird with the smell thing."

"Sorry about that, but you really do smell lovely." I winked at her; luckily she couldn't see.

"Did you just wink?"

"No, why?" I asked innocently.

Bethan nudged me playfully in the ribs, then continued. "The obvious next step is to go and talk to people at e-energy, see if they're missing personnel, or if they have any idea what's going on? But the detectives will do that and most likely uncover something, leaving me out of it."

"I'm sorry. You deserve to be there. Will it be a raid?"

"No, just some questions. Unless they don't cooperate, which I'm sure they will."

"Well, here we are. Are you heading back up?"

"No, I'm done for the day. Time to go home. Sleep well, Max, and thank you."

"Hey, it was my pleasure. Is everyone safe, Bethan? Are the people here safe? They don't seem to be taking it seriously, but I guess they don't know the full story."

"Yes, of course they're safe. I don't know what this is about yet, but I'm confident it isn't random. This has intent. Someone has an agenda here."

"Thank you. See you in the morning?" I asked, although I didn't know why.

"What do you mean?"

"Sorry, I actually don't know why I said that. I'm not part of this. I'm just a guy in the wrong place at the wrong time."

"Or the right place at the right time," she corrected.

"Maybe, but no, why would I see you in the morning? You have work, I have a nice calm walk on the beach planned. But if you are passing tomorrow and I'm around, please let me know what happened."

"Sure. No problem, Max." Bethan turned off the torch now we had the light from the farmhouse giving enough to find our way, and headed over to get her car.

Anxious and I stumbled back to Vee, half asleep. I unlocked the camper and groaned. "I broke a rule, Max. That man earlier, Mickey, told me to always ensure the bed was ready to crawl into, and look at it."

I clambered in and fought with the Rock-n-Roll bed until I got everything into position then closed the door, locked it from the inside just to be sure, and flopped onto the bed.

"Damn, I forgot to bring pillows."

It didn't matter. Anxious curled up beside me and we were both asleep in moments.

The morning brought all manner of surprises. The first one being that somehow, inexplicably, in the night we had been removed from the campervan in our sleep and transported to a furnace. It was easily a million and one degrees inside and getting hotter by the second. We both awoke gasping. Sweat dripped from me as I shot upright and banged my head on something, then groaned as I flopped back down and stared at the ceiling. Weirdly, it looked like Vee, but it certainly wasn't because of the raging, invisible conflagration all around us.

Anxious whined as he tapped my face with his paw, so I crawled forward into the tiny available space, finally found the keys in my pocket, then unlocked and opened the door. Cooler air rushed in and I discovered that, no, we weren't in some freaky kind of space-time temporal loop where we'd been transported into the heart of a volcano, but in a pleasant field with a welcome breeze drifting in from the sea to greet sleepy campers.

Anxious dove for the grass and rolled around gratefully, legs kicking in the air as he huffed with delight. I was sorely tempted to join him, but settled for just removing my socks and sliding down onto the grass with a sigh.

What was I thinking to crash on the bed with my clothes on? Apart from anything else, I'd get it dirty, and cleaning things wasn't as easy as back home. I'd totally forgotten about the need for a laundrette to do my washing, so made a vow to treat the bedding with utmost respect from now on.

"So nice and cool. Why is it so hot in there? I glanced back at the campervan and realised I had made yet another noob mistake. Not only had I not drawn the curtains for both privacy and to stop the sun's rays entering, but I'd failed to put up the folding silver foil things that came with the van. They were meant to go on the outside, I thought, or were they, to keep the temperature more stable.

Ah well, lesson learned, and no harm done. Although, there was a rather funky smell emanating from the camper. I sniffed, trying to track it down, but it followed me as I investigated. It didn't take long to realise it was me. I had neither washed nor brushed my teeth before bed, so not only did I reek, but I was still covered in soot and my mouth tasted like the inside of that cairn from yesterday.

The image of the body popped into my head, but I dismissed it. I wouldn't dwell on that. Today was for relaxing with Anxious, seeing some sights, enjoying the weather, and chilling. The police were on the case; it was nothing to do with me.

I hit the very basic showers to wash away the madness of yesterday, then used the other facilities and came out of the block feeling like a new man. Smelling like one too. I whistled as I returned to the camper with Anxious by my side. I noted Barry Simms, he of the brown clothes and matching Volvo, standing beside his car looking rather lost. His hair was wild, he was in the same outfit as yesterday, so was a crumpled, creased mess.

He seemed utterly confused, as though he didn't know what to do, or how to camp at all. What on earth was he doing here? It was obvious he was no bird-watcher. If this was a regular thing for him he'd at least have brought some provisions for the trip, but the man was clueless. Not my business.

Back at the camper, Anxious and I had breakfast. I stuck with cereal, whilst he wolfed a larger than usual bowl of dried food after the excitement of yesterday. Once everything was cleaned away and I'd wrangled the Rock-n-Roll bed back into place, I sat on the bench seat and had a nice cup of coffee. The VW might not have been the most spacious of campervans, but with the roof raised it was surprisingly roomy. You could stand with plenty of head height, and doing the dishes wasn't so bad once you got organised, but I still decided I'd invest in a few more bowls so I could do most of the washing up outside. The small fold-down seat attached to the back of the passenger seat meant it could be used as a table so I wouldn't even have to bend to do the dishes and I would have more room, so I'd go with that while the weather was good.

So, here we were. Day two of our new life. The first full day away from the old one, with the future bright and open to whatever I wished. I had transport, I had a home, I had Anxious, and I had enough money in the bank and enough coming in from the rentals to ensure I could continue this vagabond lifestyle for as long as I wished.

"Freedom!" I shouted into the clear blue sky.

People stared at me from around the campsite, but I didn't care.

"Freedom!" came voices from the far end of the field, and I spied Mickey and Sue with their fists in the air.

I waved and they waved back. Was I part of a community?

Soon enough, our words were echoing from all corners as others joined in, and I think at that precise moment I was the happiest I had ever been in my life. At least as a single man.

I pottered around for the next half hour, happy doing small tasks, organising things as I learned more about how I would use the camper, and generally having a bit of domestic rapture, which normally wasn't my thing at all. Tidying in your bare feet, wearing nothing but cut-off jeans whilst the sun shone and happy sounds flowed on the gentle breeze certainly made it an enjoyable experience rather than a chore.

Once Vee was spick and span, I called for Anxious and he hopped happily into the passenger seat. With his seatbelt secured, I settled myself then started up Vee with a pleasant low rumble. Grinning at each other, we drove across the campsite then headed towards the beach for a pleasant morning stroll on what promised to be a perfect day in paradise.

Chapter 9

The drive was hair-raising at first as I navigated the twists and turns of narrow Welsh country lanes, praying nobody would be coming in the other direction and force me to reverse. Note to self: practice reversing! The list was getting long and would only get longer, I imagined. But once out on the main routes the going was easy and the traffic light even at just gone eight in the morning.

I'd checked the directions beforehand, so didn't bother with my phone giving me instructions, and soon enough we were parked up on a headland in an official car park. It was a winding walk down a steep path to the beach, but judging by the view from up here it would be more than worth it. The sandy beach stretched east and west until lost to rocky outcroppings, a long, broad expanse perfect for a morning stroll before the tourists hit and it became crowded.

I was in a fine mood as we wandered over to the ticket machine, then it faded as I tried to figure out what on earth I was meant to do. As with all written media in Wales, everything was in both English and Welsh, so I pressed the button for English then was confronted with numerous options for my stay. After a few false starts, I thought I'd chosen a few hours and was expecting to drop in a few coins and be about my business.

But no. I needed the app. What app? I had no app for this company. Why did they all do this nowadays? Why couldn't I just use a coin? Was this a conspiracy to drive people insane? Everywhere you went you needed a different app and there was never, as here, a signal when you wanted one. I couldn't download it, I couldn't use my credit card, so resorted to putting a note in the window saying as much. As I passed through the car park, I noticed that almost every other vehicle had either something similar or no ticket displayed. The companies running these places would be making more money if they went back to good old-fashioned coins and stopped trying to modernise.

But whatever. I wasn't going to let it ruin our day. Although, I did wish I'd driven a little further where the land dipped and I could have parked right by the seafront. But the plan was to walk along the coast and get there on foot, dipping my toes in the cold water as we went.

With ball and flinger in hand, poo bags pocketed, and a smile on my face, I took the path with Anxious by my side, under strict instructions not to run off until we made it past the signs for the area where dogs weren't allowed to be off the lead. Just to be sure, I clipped his lead on when we reached the sand, even though I knew he would behave until I told him he could go play.

Past the signs warning of fines for dogs misbehaving, I unclipped him, then said, "Go on, boy!"

Anxious didn't need telling twice. With a quick glance at me to ensure he heard right, I nodded and he was off, tearing across the sand like he'd spent the last year in doggy juvie, not five minutes on a slack lead.

But oh, how glorious. The sun shone, the wind had died down, the sand was cool between my toes, and the water was still. Just gentle waves lapping at my pinkies when I braved the cool water and stood there up to my ankles, marvelling at the beauty the world had to offer to those who took the time to notice.

Anxious yapped from just in front of me, so I flung his ball out a short distance and he dove in with abandon, swimming like a pro to retrieve it.

Over and over, we repeated the game as we made our way along the beach, smiling at other walkers, saying hello to other dogs, sniffing bums—just Anxious for that particular pastime—and just having the best time ever.

The only thing that spoiled it somewhat was the ever-increasing number of green static homes that began to grow like Minecraft trees as we headed west. You saw these holiday parks everywhere around the country, full of static caravans, or weirdly called mobile homes—I could never reconcile the two, even though it meant the same thing. Long oblong buildings with all the amenities you needed, like a giant caravan or motorhome but super-sized, they were popular with families and those seeking some comfort while they enjoyed their vacation. I certainly saw the appeal, but there were just so many of them.

We moved up the beach a ways to check them out, and I was surprised to find just how busy the holiday parks were. People were enjoying themselves sitting out on decks or pottering about, children were playing, adults were chatting with neighbours and there were even a few early morning barbecues. Hey, they were on holiday and who could blame them on such a fine day with the incredible views right on their plastic doorstep? The owners must have been making a fortune.

In between two such places was a field with tents and several motorhomes, almost like the campsite was being eaten up by the green boxes, and I wondered how it had looked a few years ago. I guess the money was in the larger sites that offered more amenities, rather than the prices you could charge for pitching a tent.

But still, they were relatively tastefully done and not too cramped, and people were relaxed and happy, so good luck to them.

We continued on our way, the holiday parks fading into fields and sand dunes, even a golf course. Holidaymakers were beginning to get set up for the day now, but I knew the real busy period was yet to come in August when the children all over the UK got their six-week summer holiday. Beaches up and down the country would be rammed with families cramming in as much sun as they could get in the ever-changeable British climate.

We had what, six or seven weeks before school was out for summer, so I made a mental note to hit as many beaches as we could before possibly heading inland for a while to explore, or maybe seek out some quieter spots. But that was a long ways off yet. We had the entire Welsh coastline to explore, then down to Cornwall, which I definitely wanted to visit before the tourist season got into full swing.

Once we hit the main part of the beach most tourists would use, where the parking made the beach accessible and the numerous shops were close by, I put Anxious back on the lead just to be safe, and headed up to the road. I stopped dead in my tracks when I spied Volvo Barry pointing his camera at us. He quickly changed direction when he realised I'd spotted him, scanning the horizon like he wasn't spying on me, but I got a tingle down my spine and wondered what his game was.

I strode towards him but he glanced my way and lowered his camera then stood from the bench and began to walk off.

"Barry. Barry!" I called, then picked up the pace and called his name again.

He stopped, then started again, until with a sag of the shoulders he turned and smiled at me. He waited while I caught up with him, then beamed, his lank hair already plastered to his scalp with sweat. "Out for some exercise, eh?" he asked.

"Yes, you too?"

"Couldn't miss such a beautiful morning."

"You seemed to be watching me," I said, forgoing my usual polite nature because this guy just screamed wrong on so many levels.

"Watching you?" he frowned. "No, I was scanning for birds, and I did see you, but I wasn't watching you. Why would I be?"

"I don't know. Sorry, I think I'm just jittery after what happened yesterday. Did you hear?"

"Yes, terrible business. A body in the road. How awful. The police asked if I'd seen anything, but it was news to me. What about you?"

"I'm the one who found the poor man. It was very upsetting."

"I bet."

I watched him closely, wondering again if it might be him, but he didn't seem the type to commit multiple murders, although he did give me the creeps.

"Did the police say what they think happened? Was it murder?" His eyes widened, but his body language suggested he knew only too well it was murder.

"Yes, I assume it was murder. But I guess that's down to the police to figure out." I kept quiet about the other body, not wanting to mention it for some reason.

"Of course. Best leave them to it. You don't want to get involved in such awful things."

"No, I don't. So, what are your plans? You seem to be very under-prepared for camping. You get the tent up alright?" I asked innocently.

Barry coughed at the mention and blurted, "You saw, didn't you?"

"I might have taken a peek at you putting it up. I didn't want to interfere, as you looked like you were having such a great time."

Barry smiled, a genuine smile, as he said, "Gee, thanks. Next time you see me struggling, feel free to help."

"So, you staying long?"

"Just a few days, I expect. I have some free time, so figured why not? I need to get supplies, and clothes, though, but it's worth it. It's lovely here." Barry tugged at his crumpled shirt and frowned, then his eyes drifted to the shops lining the road, most likely wondering what clothes were available for a man with a definite obsession for all things brown. There was an unmistakable Geography teacher vibe about him. Maybe he was?

"You don't need to get back to work? Are you a teacher?"

"A teacher? Whatever gave you that idea? No, I'm a freelance writer. Copywriting, that kind of thing. I can work anywhere, but I have nothing urgent and I can just use the laptop if I need to. Shame there's no internet at the campsite, but it's actually kind of refreshing being back to basics."

"I hear that. I'm loving it. Well, see you around." I waved, then wandered towards the shops. As I turned, he quickly moved his camera in another direction. What was with this guy? I couldn't figure him out at all.

I stocked up on a few things for the next couple of days, taking my time perusing the shelves of a small Tesco and enjoying myself no end. I never did things like this, and it was an utter novelty. Having been a chef for so many years, the restaurant food was either delivered or from our own animals and gardens, and food at home was invariably leftovers from work, or whatever Min had prepared. She got home delivery, so I couldn't recall the last time either of us had set foot in a supermarket until I'd got supplies to come away.

With a few choice items chosen for my one-pot feast that evening, and bits and pieces I'd failed to think of before the trip began, plus the all-important washing up bowls, I paid then hurried to untie Anxious who was waiting patiently outside, doing a spot of people watching.

"Time to get back and relax, I think," I told him.

He yawned, so we walked back to the van slowly then drove home. It was weird to think of a random campsite as home, but there it was, my new outlook. Home was wherever the van was to be for the day.

The drive through the woods was as spooky as ever, and I was glad to emerge into daylight. I pulled up at the gate to the campsite and jumped out to open it, pausing when I heard a commotion. The three incongruous men from yesterday, the two bruisers and the smaller one who seemed to somehow be their boss, were outside the cottage talking with Dai.

Dai was ranting and looked beyond angry as he shook his fists at the smaller man and pointed to the gate. He saw me, but the others didn't even turn, then the two bodyguards, even more intimidating when standing next to an old man, closed in on him in a very menacing way. The boss put a hand to each of their shoulders and said something, so they took a step back. He held his hands out to placate Dai, but the old farmer was clearly incensed about something and continued to fume.

With a final word, then a cheery wave, the boss and his goons walked idly over to their black Range Rover then the door was opened for the boss who got into the back and the two meatballs got in up front.

I drove through the gate then pulled up alongside and asked if they were heading out. The goon just nodded without speaking, so I waited for them to leave then turned the engine off and closed the gate as they hadn't bothered.

Dai looked upset, and was visibly shaking, so I wandered over and asked, "Everything alright? A bit of bother?"

"Those damn idiots won't leave me alone. They think they can intimidate me, but they're wrong. I don't scare easily, no matter what they try."

"Did they have something to do with the murders?" I asked, incredulous.

"What?" snapped Dai, distracted. "No, at least I don't think so. The police spoke to them, same as everyone else. A few people have left because of it, but most don't seem too concerned. Guess they would be if they knew the whole story though. Those men are from the Happy Valleys Corporation. That little fella is the chairman, if you can believe such a thing. They're buying up all the land they can along the coast and turning it into those holiday park things. There won't be a campsite left at this rate."

"I saw a few today down by the sea. They own them all?"

"Aye, they do. They offer people a price it's hard to refuse, and most sell up. Some don't, but they drive people out, make it hard to earn a living, and sooner or later most cave. You can't fight big business, is what I hear everyone saying. But I can. And I will."

"But you don't think they had anything to do with the murders?"

"I wouldn't put it past them. You saw those brutes he had with him. They're dirty players and will do anything to undermine people's business so they can swoop in and take it off their hands. But I'm just venting. People don't commit murder to buy a campsite."

"People do all sorts of crazy stuff, Dai. What did they say to you?"

"Just made me an offer like they do every week. I didn't realise who they were when they arrived. I'd never seen them before. In the past it was just some lackey, but I guess they figured it was time to bring out the big guns to intimidate the old man. It didn't work. They offered a fair price, but I'm not selling. This is my home and has been in the family for generations. One day it will be Bethan's, and nobody's taking that girl's inheritance from her. Her folks aren't the type to run a campsite, and aren't the best at business, but she loves it. When I go, it'll be hers."

"Sorry you had to deal with all that. You okay?"

"Aye, lad, I'm fine. You settling in alright?"

"Um, yes, kind of. You know about yesterday? What Bethan and I discovered?"

"Sure I do. Don't you fret about it. Nothing to worry about." He dismissed it with a wave, like it was nothing more than a minor issue.

"Dai, it's two dead bodies right on your doorstep. Aren't you concerned?"

"Not really. I'm sure the police will sort this mess out. You just focus on enjoying your time here. If you need anything, don't hesitate not to come see me."

"Um, don't you mean don't hesitate to come see you?"

"No, I don't," he said gruffly, back to being the cantankerous Welsh farmer I got the feeling he enjoyed playing when he was feeling mischievous.

Dai winked at me and I laughed, then nodded and got back into the camper.

Time to relax a while then think about lunch.

Chapter 10

"Mum? Dad? What on earth are you doing here?"

Anxious barked happily and dashed over to my parents, wagging excitedly as he jumped up at them and they made a fuss of him.

I walked over to join them, giving Mum a kiss and Dad a hearty handshake, then stepped back to take in my utterly bonkers parents. Children of the late sixties, they were now in their mid-fifties and, bizarrely, that's the era they'd both been stuck in ever since they were teenagers.

They met each other at a fifties swing night, as they were both obsessed with the music, fashion, and icons of the nineteen-fifties. Both were still as much in love with the era as they were with each other even after so many years.

Dad wore his usual Teddy boy outfit of indigo denim jeans with fat turn-ups, a white muscle T-shirt with the sleeves rolled up to show off his biceps, and slicked back greasy hair a la John Travolta from Grease. Yes, it was their favourite movie.

Mum, and I had to admit she looked good, sported a polka dot wide hemmed dress, bright red dyed hair, dark eye make-up, plenty of blusher on her pale skin, and a black and white bandana over her forehead to keep the hair from her eyes. They looked like they were off to a dance, not trudging around a campsite in Rhyl.

"We were worried," said Mum with a frown, before she caught me in her Mum arm net and held me tight.

"We were, Son," agreed Dad with a shake of the head. He mouthed a silent, "Sorry," followed by a shrug.

I got it. Mum was concerned, Dad tried to convince her not to come, but she insisted.

"I'm fine. I only left yesterday. It's rather soon to be fretting, isn't it? What on earth made you come? I'm an adult, you know? I can look after myself."

"You didn't call or message last night," said Mum, shaking her head.

"I told you it was likely there wouldn't be a signal."

"What about wi-fi?"

"They don't have it here. It's an old fella running things and he never said anything about wi-fi. Although, come to think of it they take internet bookings so he probably has it."

"Then you should have emailed. Or done that other thing on your phone."

"WhatsApp?"

"Nothing. I'm fine. Why?"

"No, WhatsApp, the way we message on our phones sometimes."

"Yes, dear, of course," said Mum, dismissing it immediately like she did anything she didn't understand.

"Look, it's awesome to see you, but did you seriously drive all this way to check on me? I left yesterday. I saw you yesterday."

"Son, just go with it," said Dad with a slap on my back. "Your mum was worried when we didn't hear, and we fancied a day trip anyway. We thought we'd come visit then leave you to it. Don't worry, we won't cramp your style."

"What style?" laughed Mum as she looked me up and down, scowling at my cutoffs and vest. She focused on my Crocs, rubbed her eyes in disbelief, checked again, then gasped as her eyes bulged. "No son of mine should wear those things! Did you go out in public with them on? Did anyone see you? You didn't tell them we were related, did you?"

"We're at a campsite. Everyone wears them. They dry out in seconds if you get them wet, and they're great for the beach. You can paddle in them if it's rocky, the sand doesn't stick, and they're the most comfortable thing I've ever worn."

"You look like a hippy."

"Good, because I feel like one," I laughed, winking at Dad.

"Put the kettle on, Son. I'm parched. It was a long drive. Especially with these two nattering."

"These two?" I asked, confused.

"Where is she?" asked Dad, frowning.

"She went to the loo. She was bursting," said Mum with a roll of her eyes.

"Oh yes, I forgot."

"Who are you talking about?" I asked, utterly confounded now.

"Here she is," said Mum brightly.

I turned to follow her gaze and saw Min waving brightly, halfway across the field. "You brought Min?"

"Yes. Actually," confided Mum with a sly wink, "it was her idea."

"It was?" I asked, grinning.

"Yes, it was, Son," whispered Dad. "She called us last night, saying she hadn't heard, and asked if we had. When she discovered we hadn't, she suggested we come and check on you. I think it was an excuse as she misses you. Don't blow it, Son."

"I've already blown it. Over a year ago, remember?"

"We remember," sighed Mum. "You stupid boy. She's the best thing that ever happened to you and you messed it up. It was like losing our only child."

"Yes, thank you for reminding me. I'd forgotten entirely about how I screwed up my life and hers. Glad you brought it up. And in case you've forgotten, I'm your only child."

"No need to get snappy," warned Mum.

"Play it cool," suggested Dad. "Here she comes. Don't tell her we said it was her idea. Pretend we cajoled her. That's what we agreed so she wouldn't feel silly."

"Why would she feel silly?"

"Because she doesn't want to care, but she does. Because she misses you and we miss her too. She's like the daughter we never had and we want her back."

"That's not going to happen," I said.

"No?" asked Dad. "Then why'd she drag us all the way up here the day after you left? If she didn't care, she wouldn't have done that."

"What are you whispering about?" asked Min with a beautiful smile I liked to think was just for me.

"Nothing at all," said Mum, looking so innocent she looked entirely guilty of numerous untold crimes.

"Good," said Min. "Well, aren't you going to say hello?" she asked me.

"Of course. Great to see you." We pecked each other on the cheek while Mum and Dad pretended not to look, even though Mum went, "Ah," so stepped back from each other and smiled.

"I was worried," said Min.

Anxious pawed at her legs, incensed at being ignored even for a moment, so Min bent and gave him a huge fuss, laughing as he rolled over for a tummy tickle.

"There was no need. I'm fine. Anxious is fine. Vee is fine."

"Vee? You have another woman? I knew I shouldn't have come," blurted Min, face reddening. "I'm so sorry. Is she inside? We'll leave. I'll leave. This was a bad idea. I'm such an idiot."

"Min, calm down. Of course there isn't another woman. You know there won't be."

"Not with that outfit on, and those crimes against shoes on your feet," said Mum.

I ignored her, and carried on. "It's the name for the campervan. Not very original, I know, but I call her Vee. Because she's a VW."

"Oh, yes," Min laughed nervously as she stood and Anxious sniffed the ground around us in case anyone had brought treats. "Right! Oops. Not that there would be anything wrong if you did have someone here. You're single, and I have no right to tell you what to do. It's perfectly fine."

Mum placed a hand on her shoulder and said, "I think you better stop there, love. We all know you still adore the dopey lad."

"I'm not a lad. I'm thirty-three. But what do you mean she still adores me? Min?"

"Of course I do," she mumbled. "It's obvious, isn't it? But we weren't right for each other and it went sour. But this last year you've changed. Me too. I know it's too late, we're divorced, but I still care about you."

"And I care about you. Thanks for coming. Although, and you all have to admit this, it's beyond weird."

"You're weird," blurted Mum.

"I'll put the kettle on, shall I?" I asked, just to get some space to process things.

"Let me help," said Min. "I can see *Vee* in action. She better be treating you right."

"Oh she is. We had the best night's sleep. Once I got the Rock-n-Roll bed sorted. I learned a load of cool tips yesterday from this guy but forgot the cardinal rule of sorting out the bed early. It was quite a weird and long day, actually."

"Did someone say rock-and-roll?" asked Dad, peering inside the camper then striking an Elvis pose.

"The bed, Dad. It's called a Rock-n-Roll bed."

"Wouldn't mind one of those myself," he mumbled, then withdrew and left us alone.

With the kettle on, Min and I sat on the bench seat while Mum and Dad played with Anxious. Min was quiet, uncharacteristically so, and I don't know what possessed me but I took her hand. She closed her fingers around mine and we sat there like that, neither of us speaking until the kettle began to whistle.

I jumped up and turned it off.

"What are we doing, Max? This is ridiculous. I'm ridiculous."

"You are not ridiculous. You're amazing."

"See, that's the problem. You shouldn't be talking like that about your ex-wife who you lost your home and half your money to."

"I gave it willingly. It was the least I could do."

"But it's not right. It's not how people do things. We should be fighting, arguing, bitter and twisted."

"You should be bitter for what I put you through."

"I've told you, it wasn't just you. I was just as bad. Never around, never there for you. I could have helped, done more for you. Encouraged you to take a step back."

"Min, let's not go over it again. What's done is done. If I could go back and do it all over again, you can bet I would, and I'd do it differently."

"Me too."

"I still can't believe you came. And with Mum and Dad. What were you thinking?"

"I honestly don't know," she laughed, brushing her hair from her face and settling her blue eyes on mine. "It was the longest trip of my life. We listened to fifties music the whole way. And they sang, Max. To every single song. For hours."

"Welcome to my world. Imagine what it was like when I was young. But they like you, sometimes even more than me. We all miss you. Anxious does too."

"And I miss him terribly. How's he been?"

"He's loving it. Although, this is only the second day, and yesterday was..."

"What? Didn't it go well? Problems with the camper?"

"Not really, no. There was an, er, incident."

"Tell me," she demanded, eyes dancing with intrigue.

"Let me make the drinks, then I will. But I'm still surprised you guys are here. I'm not being very independent and having a wild man adventure if my ex-wife and parents arrive on what's basically day one."

"Shall we go?"

"Don't you dare!"

Once the tea was made, we took it outside and I set up seating as best I could for everyone. Mum and Dad had the camp chairs, we made do with an upturned storage box for a table, while Min and I took a blanket.

"So, this is nice," I said. "At least, I think it is. But there's something you all should know."

"I knew it," said Mum. "He's got into trouble already."

"Mum, I'm a grown man who ran the kitchens of numerous successful, top-rated restaurants. I'm more than capable of looking after myself and not getting into trouble."

"Sorry, love. So what happened?"

"There was a murder."

"What!" gasped Mum. "See, I told you we shouldn't let him go off on his own. Now look what's happened," she told Dad.

"Doubt he did it," said Dad, shaking his head. "Carry on, Son."

"Actually, it seems like there were two murders."

"He's going to be next!" screeched Mum. "Right, pack your bags. You're coming home with us right now."

"Don't be daft. I have the van if I want to go anywhere. But I'm not leaving. Let me explain."

It took a while. In fact, it took two cups of tea, a pack and a half of biscuits, several tissues for Mum, and a lot of repeating what I'd just said as Mum interrupted incessantly and Dad was a little deaf in one ear even though he refused to admit it. Min rested her hand on my knee the whole time and squeezed it now and then. I could have stayed there for eternity.

"Sounds like gangsters to me," said Mum.

"More like some numpty who got tangled in his tent," said Dad.

"What about the skeleton in the cairn?" I asked.

"Probably been there for years and has nothing to do with it."

"Then how do you explain the boiler suit up the chimney and the rags in with the skeleton?" I asked, intrigued.

"Simple," smirked Dad, running his hands over his slicked-back hair. "Someone found them somewhere, decided to use them to block the chimney so no smoke would be seen while they had a tiny fire, and left it there. Probably some got taken by animals and dragged into the cairn."

"No, you wouldn't stuff one up a chimney. It might catch fire," said Min.

"So what's your answer?" asked Dad, put out.

"That someone's going around killing e-energy employees and is utterly psycho."

"What about the clothes up the chimney? Why would you do that?" I asked.

"To hide them, of course."

"But they were filthy. You'd never put them on again."

"Maybe you would if you were planning on going back up the chimney," said Min smugly.

"You're right! I never even thought about that. I wonder if the detectives checked."

"Doubt it," said Dad. "They might have shone a torch up the chimney, same as your new lady friend did, but I doubt they'd have checked further than they could see. Most chimneys have a crook in them. Could you see right up to the top?"

"No, it did bend. We never thought to check higher. And she isn't my lady friend. She's a police officer."

"Is she pretty?" asked Dad with a wink. He loved making me uncomfortable.

"Hadn't noticed. And even if she was, and smelled absolutely bloody lovely, she's young enough to be my daughter. Well, almost, but I'd have had to be really young when I had her."

"Oh, giving birth now, are we?" asked Mum with a glare. "Decided to take that away from us, have you? Want to take credit for the miracle of childbirth?"

"No, of course not! I was just saying, she's very young. Quite new to the force. We bumped into each other at the cottage and discovered the body and the clues. She was very helpful."

"I bet she was," said Dad with a wink.

"And how nice did she smell?" teased Min.

"Not as nice as you," I grinned, leaning in and sniffing her neck, my lips almost touching her warm, familiar skin. I shouldn't have done it. It was too personal, and she pulled away. "Sorry, that was out of order."

"Let's go take a look," said Dad, coming to my rescue.

"At what?"

"The chimney, of course."

"It was fine," mumbled Min, then squeezed my knee as she smiled demurely.

What was happening? Why was she acting so... How was she acting? Was I reading this wrong, or was something actually going on here?

"Hello? Earth to son." Dad waved his hand in front of my face and I came back down with a very parental bump.

"Sorry, I was miles away."

"Dreaming of necks," muttered Mum with a very dramatic tut.

"Was not!"

Mum gave me a knowing smile. She'd love for us to get back together, and was merely trying to stop me making a fool of myself.

"So, the chimney," suggested Dad. "Let's go take a look."

"I don't think we can. It's a crime scene. There was a body up there, remember? The police are most likely still going through things. Sifting through evidence, forensics, that kind of thing."

"Don't be daft, you silly sod. This isn't a cop show. This is rural Wales. They'll have gone to bed last night, had a crack at it this morning, then cleared out. Probably already off down the boozer, then they'll have an afternoon nap."

"How would you know?"

"Just trust your dad," said Mum.

"That's right, you should trust me. And besides, we need to walk Anxious."

"He had a massive one this morning. We went to the beach. And I haven't even told you about that yet, or the weird characters I met yesterday or what I saw this morning. There's something very odd about this place, and people are up to no good."

"Then you can tell us all about it while we have a walk. What's for lunch?"

"I didn't know you were coming, so there's nothing for lunch."

"Great! We'll hit the shops after we have our walk."

"Will you stop saying that! Look at the state of him. You know better than to say the W word in front of Anxious."

Anxious was spinning in circles with excitement, each mention of the word building on the last until he was close to a meltdown. Never mind that he could run around freely, we'd been to the beach and he was exhausted, and he'd had a swim, Anxious never tired of adventure and thought every walk was going to be the best one ever; the one where he'd finally catch himself a rabbit.

Dad ignored me and stood, then looked down at Anxious who was now sitting at his feet, staring with hope in his eyes and his tail brushing the grass so hard he was wearing it away to bare ground.

"You want to go for a little walk up the hill, Anxious?" asked Dad with a wicked smirk at me.

Anxious barked and barked until I relented and said, "Fine, but I'm telling you, the police will be there. And how's Mum going to get up there? High heels are not the correct footwear."

"I came prepared," said Mum smugly, then pulled out a pair of walking boots from the bag for life I hadn't even noticed she was carrying.

"What else do you have in there?" I asked, suddenly suspicious.

"Just things. Essentials," she mumbled.

"Like?"

"Make-up, a brush. Some clean underwear for you."

"I knew it! You are one crazy old lady. I'm an adult. I don't need clean underwear."

"Everyone needs clean underwear, Son," chided Dad. "You don't want to be known as Skid Marks Max."

"Sometimes you say the weirdest things, Dad. Why would anyone ever call me that? No, don't answer. I meant, I have my own underwear. Although, are they Marks and Sparks?"

"Of course," huffed Mum, affronted. "Where else could you possibly buy underwear apart from Marks and Spencers?"

Everyone agreed there was nowhere else, and with that settled we waited while Mum changed into her boots then set off up the hill.

Chapter 11

"I can't believe you came," I whispered to Min as we hiked up the trail with Anxious so close to her she risked tripping over the excited guy.

"Neither can I. It's great to see you, Anxious," she said rather loudly, then bent and patted him before straightening and continuing up the hill.

"Why did you come?"

"Honestly, I don't know. I guess after you being so different this last year without the stress of work, I wanted to see for myself how you were handling things away from everything."

"On day two? I saw you yesterday."

"Are you teasing me?"

"Maybe a little. I'm so pleased you're here, Min. I didn't expect this. Everything okay at home?"

"Yes, fine. Okay, I admit it, I'm jealous and wanted to find you at your worst so I could see what it would be like to go it alone. As I said, I'm jealous."

"Of what?" I asked, confused. "Not me giving everything up?"

"Of you. You finally did it. Something you've been talking about for ages. You sorted everything out and did it. Remember when this was our dream? To do it together? We used to have weekends away if we both had a lull at work, but there was always the stress and worry hanging over us. Now you don't have that. You're finally free. You did it and I'm jealous."

"You could have done it if you wanted to."

"I know, but I'm a coward. I can't seem to face packing in my job once and for all and enjoying things for a while. Maybe I'm scared of my life being too quiet. Too much time to think. I know I shouldn't complain, as who else my age has the luxury of even choosing between working or not, but there you have it. I have the choice but I can't quit, and I'm jealous that you've done something so brave."

"You'll figure it out. One thing I learned from the crap we went through is that life is too short. Even if you mess up for years and years, it's never too late. Better to try and fail, than never to try, right?"

"Right. Maybe I will quit. Become a homeless vagabond like you and spend my life in awful cut-off jeans and sad Crocs."

"There is nothing wrong with Crocs!" I exclaimed, raising my hands. "You should get a pair. They're beyond comfortable. And I thought the shorts looked good. My knees aren't that knobbly, are they?"

"No, your knees are fine. I'm just messing with you, Max. Now, what's really been going on here?"

"How'd you mean?"

"I mean, there's more than you told your folks. I know that much. What am I missing out on?"

"Nothing much. The only thing I didn't mention was this weird guy further down the field who turned up yesterday without even a tent. I think he's watching me. He's odd."

"Why would he be watching you? Do you think he's the killer?"

"I doubt it, and I'm not even sure if he is spying on me. Maybe he's just a pervert. Or... I just don't know. But it's not important. Look, here we are."

We waited for Mum and Dad to catch us up, then approached the cottage.

Min was overexcited by the quaint setup, especially when I told her the story of Old Mrs. Jones who'd lived here her whole life. She couldn't wait to go inside.

"Guys, I don't think we should. Remember what I said about this being a crime scene? We don't want to screw anything up."

"Then where's the coppers stopping us?" asked Dad, pulling his comb from the back pocket of his Levi's and running the steel through his hair.

"Guess the police didn't think anyone would come up here."

"You did," said Mum.

"True. Look, this just doesn't feel right. And anyway, how are we going to get down the chimney?"

"We don't get down the chimney, you numpty," said Dad with a woeful shake of his head.

"No?"

"No. Have you learned nothing in you thirty whatever it is years?"

"You don't know how old I am, do you?"

"Course I do! You were born in, um, nineteen..."

"Yes?"

"Nineteen... ninety... or, er, eighty..."

"Getting warmer," I said.

"Anyway, you should know how to deal with this problem."

"Dad, I can say with my hand on my heart that I have never had to try to possibly recover a maybe clue from a chimney before."

"Maybe you should have!" Everyone stared at Dad. "What? I'm just saying. Come on, follow me."

Dad brushed past me, all business, and marched into the cottage like he owned it. We hurried after him, and I bumped into his back where he'd paused in the cramped hallway.

"What are you doing?" I hissed.

"Nothing. Just getting a sense of the place. Does it feel cold to you? Did you hear something?"

"Of course it's cooler. They built them to stay cool during summer, warm in winter. It's the stone walls."

"No, I didn't mean that. I mean, what if there's a ghost?" Dad shivered.

"Are you serious?" I laughed. "Come on, it's in here." I led the way into the main room and Dad reluctantly followed, allowing Mum, Min, and Anxious to enter too.

"Cool inglenook," gushed Min. "I always wanted one."

"She used to do all her cooking here. She even made bread in those little ovens built into the walls. Pretty clever, eh?"

"It really is."

"So, where'd you find your clue, Son?" asked Dad, seemingly over his heebie-jeebies.

"It was wedged right up in the chimney. Bethan managed to reach it, and she's even shorter than Mum."

"I am not short. I'm just not tall."

"Short, you mean," said Dad with a wink at me and Min.

Mum tutted but smiled. She knew nobody was trying to be mean.

"So, what's the plan?" I asked Dad. "But maybe we should just tell the police?"

"Don't be a plonker, Son. Why would we do that?"

"So they can ensure no evidence is contaminated. So we don't risk letting a killer get away with this. You know, unimportant things like that."

"Sometimes you are an utter pilchard."

"Don't you call my boy a pilchard," warned Mum.

"Well he is. What kind of man won't search for evidence of a murder up a chimney and worry about upsetting some local coppers? He's a pilchard."

"You do know how utterly ridiculous you sound, right?" I sighed, wondering if I was adopted as I absolutely hated swing, Doo-wop, and most fifties music and would rather chop off my arm, beat myself over the head with it, then stomp on the mushy remains than slick back my hair and have a duck's arse at the back of my head.

"Pilchard," muttered Dad.

"Go on then, Mr. Smarty Pants. How will you search for this mystery clue?" goaded Mum.

"What's going on in here?" barked a familiar voice from the doorway. "Police. Stop what you're doing. Everyone put their hands up. I said, FREEZE!"

Mum and Dad turned, then their arms shot up, Min, for some inexplicable reason, dropped onto the floor and spread-eagled, and I just smiled at Bethan as she winked at me, her hands clasped together in her familiar I-have-deadly-fingers-and-know-how-to-use-them pose.

Nobody said a word, and it began to get weird.

"Er, guys, you know she's just pointing her fingers at you, right?" I said several seconds later when Bethan still hadn't moved and neither had anyone else.

"Hey, don't spoil it," whined Bethan. "That beats my record by three seconds. I've never had anyone take so long to realise I didn't have a gun. And it's my first spread-eagle. Hello, by the way. Everyone can relax. Unless," she warned, cocking her finger and pointing her hands at them again, causing Mum and Dad to put their arms back up and Min to drop to the sooty floor once more, "you're all... murderers!" she hissed dramatically. If she had the means, I'm sure she would have played some *dum, dum, dum* music.

"Everyone, this is Bethan. Bethan, this is everyone."

"Oh, hello there, love," cooed Mum as she lowered her arms and rushed over then gave Bethan a cuddle.

"Lovely to meet you," gushed Dad, then shoved Mum out of the way and pinched the squirming police officer's cheeks.

"Dad, she's a police constable. You can't pinch her cheeks like she's a little girl."

"She's still a woman, and women love that," admonished Dad.

"They really don't," said Bethan with a wince as she rubbed her now rosy cheeks. "That's a criminal offence. I'm afraid I'll have to take you down to the station and charge you. It's a minimum sentence these days as it's classed as sexual assault, so you're looking at jail time of at least six months."

Dad blanched and his legs buckled beneath him. He dropped to his knees and screamed, "I didn't mean it. Max made me do it. It was him. Take him instead. I'm old, he's still a lad. It was him. Criminal," he wailed, pointing at me.

"Remind me never to commit a crime with you," I grumbled, then winked at Bethan and mouthed a silent, "Nice work."

Bethan giggled, Mum tutted at her weak-in-the-face-of-authority husband, and Min finally decided to get up from the floor.

Anxious watched with his head cocked, no doubt wondering what on earth was wrong with humans and how come they managed to be the ones in charge when they were clearly all utter idiots.

"Up you get," Bethan told Dad.

He looked up and asked, "I'm not going to jail?"

"No, of course not. Just my little joke. You can see I don't have a gun, right?"

"Um, now you mention it. You surprised me. It all happened so fast. Did you see anything, love?" he asked Mum.

"No. I thought she was going to shoot us."

"And Min was too busy licking the flagstones," I laughed.

"I was not," she huffed, brushing herself down. "I thought that was what we were meant to do."

"She said 'hands up,' not 'lie down and lick soot,'" I giggled, unable to help myself.

"Aren't you going to introduce us properly, Son?" asked Dad. He was old-fashioned in some ways, like a kid in others, but he took knowing who he was talking to seriously.

"Yes, of course. Min, this is Police Constable Bethan Jones. The best policewoman this side of the border. Or do I say police officer?"

"Nice to meet you," said Min.

"And you," said Bethan. "And you're meant to say police officer, but I'm good with policewoman, because that's what I am. A woman and a police." She mulled that ever for a moment, then frowned and added, "Something like that, anyway."

It was fascinating to watch as both women eyed each other up, taking the measure of the other in a second or two. Bethan was all smiles and radiated the innocence of youth, while Min seemed suspicious, as though... I wasn't really sure, but could it be she was jealous of the time I'd spent with Bethan and the fact she was so young and smelled so lovely?

"Can I have a sniff?" asked Dad, totally wrecking the introductions.

Before Bethan could protest, he stepped forward, crouched, and sniffed from her waist right up to the top of her head. He nodded sagely, turned, and said, "You were right, Son. She smells cracking."

"Sorry about the idiot in denim," I said to Bethan. "They only let him out of the hospital today and he has no idea how to act around anyone not in a straight jacket."

"Oi, I was just sayin'."

"Well don't, you stupid man," tutted Mum. "Lovely to meet you, Bethan. I'm Jill, and that fool is Jack."

"Bethan," said Bethan totally unnecessarily. Something clicked in her head and she asked, "So, you're Jack and Jill, and they're Max and Min?"

"That's right, love. Why do you ask?" said Mum, still after all this time oblivious to the comedy names we shared. She never did get it when I moaned about my given name, saying it was lovely and meant I was destined to be a real go-getter.

"No reason. They're just so nice."

"Aren't they though?" said Mum, beaming. "Now, is there anything we can do for you, love?" she asked like she owned the place. "We're rather busy."

"Yes, actually," began Bethan, casting a bemused look my way. "I was wondering why you were here? I came to check on a few things, and I don't think you're meant to be here."

"There was no tape across the door," said Dad. "No tape means you're allowed. It's the law."

"That absolutely isn't true," I muttered.

"I guess nobody thought there was anything else to find," said Bethan.

"So what happened? Any news?" I asked.

Bethan glanced around at everyone, then said, "I don't suppose if I tell you privately you'll keep it to yourself?"

"What do you think?" I laughed. "Mum will roast me over a fire until I squeal."

"Just a teensy one," agreed Mum.

"Fine, but this stays between us," sighed Bethan.

We agreed that we'd keep schtum, so Bethan said, "They took the skeleton away in bags. Quite a few, but they were missing a few bones. Most likely the animals got them."

"Badgers ate his face off," I explained.

Mum urged, Dad muttered something about bloody badgers, blaming that bloke from Queen for making everyone have to listen to the badger song and it ruining his radio, and Min gasped.

"Nobody said badgers ate his face," warned Bethan. "Although they might have had a nibble on his toes. Anyway, the coroner's office has the remains and a pathologist will be checking them over after the body Max found yesterday. There's still no news about it, although from what the detectives said, there won't be anything to find. There were no marks on the body that could have killed him."

"What about e-energy?" I asked.

"A load of detectives went down to the local branch this morning to interview the staff and whoever is in charge. They came back complaining about them being a right bunch of know-it-alls who refused to help. All they got were a few curt replies, but not much help. But they got a list of employees and me and a few others have spent the morning trying to track them down. I spoke to a few installers and they all said the same thing. None of their guys are unaccounted for. They go through training and the money's good, so most stick with e-energy as they pay better than anyone else."

"So what's your theory?" asked Dad.

"Who says I have one?"

"Come on. I can tell you're a smart woman. You have a theory."

"Fine, but you have to promise not to speak about this with anyone. Gosh, I can't believe I'm sharing this with you. It's totally not allowed. Swear you'll never tell. My theory is that someone stole the boiler suits and was impersonating an installer to gain access to people's homes. Beyond that, I simply don't know. We have no idea who either of the men are. There's no ID, nothing to identify them. So far, it's a dead end."

"And that's why you're here, isn't it?" I said knowingly.

"What do you mean?" asked Bethan.

"You got an idea. Same as we did."

"What idea?"

"On three?"

Bethan nodded.

"One. Two. Three."

"There's something up the chimney!" we both blurted, then laughed.

"You had the same idea?" asked Bethan.

"Actually, Dad did."

"I did," he said, puffing out his chest with pride.

"And how were you going to check?"

"That's easy," he said, rubbing his hands together.

Five minutes later, I was in a position I never thought I'd be in.

Dad and I were in the inglenook. I was sitting on his shoulders and poking up the chimney with my arm, following the bend in the soot-covered walls and tearing my nails on the ancient stone. I reached up as high as I could and felt something with the tips of my fingers.

"Stand on tip-toe," I told Dad. He lifted me a little higher and I managed to get my hand around something hard but slightly warm, possibly wood, then grabbed it tight and yanked. It released with a cloud of soot, leaving me coughing and Dad retching so hard that he wobbled about and I cracked my head on the chimney.

"Someone come and catch this so I can get down," I called.

"Ready," said Bethan.

I released the item, clambered down off Dad, and dashed out into the main space, gasping, then exited through the front door and sucked in air as my father joined me, looking like a chimney sweep from the olden days.

"This better be worth it, Son," he grumbled as he took out his comb.

"It was your idea!"

"Don't get smart. Look at my jeans!"

"I'd worry more about the rest of you," I grimaced, teasing a twig from my hair.

The others came out to join us and we crowded around as Bethan held out a simple wooden box.

Chapter 12

"Let's take it out of the shade where there's more light and the air's better," said Bethan.

We dutifully followed the young officer into the sunshine, then crowded round as she sat on the wall and rested the box in her lap.

Dad did an emergency comb of his hair, causing soot to fall like malevolent dandruff, which set him off on a sneezing fit. Everyone waited for him to get his act together, then we leaned in close as Bethan sucked in air then lifted the lid of the dark box.

"ID badges," grunted Bethan as she lifted her head and met our eyes.

Dad reached in to grab one, but Mum slapped his hand and tutted.

"Ow! What did you do that for?" Dad glared at her, but she doubled his glare and raised him a triple tut. He didn't stand a chance and was out.

"Everyone knows you don't touch evidence. Now who's the pilchard?"

Much to Dad's chagrin, everyone agreed that he most definitely was the prize pilchard now as it was amateur sleuthing 101 to never contaminate the scene.

Bethan slipped on a pair of disposable gloves and carefully lifted out the pile of identity badges. They were e-energy ones, laminated and on lanyards to slip over your neck. She shuffled through them, grunting at names, holding them up to the light and generally looking very professional. Then she grinned at us, shook her hair which sent a waft of her perfume to flowing like a lily freshly blooming on a summer's day, and everyone sighed.

"You really do smell lovely," admitted Min.

"Like summer," agreed Mum.

"Told you," Dad and I crowed.

"Um, thanks." Bethan smiled despite herself. "You know what this means, don't you?"

"That you spend lots on perfume?" asked Dad, rather slow on the uptake.

"She's talking about the IDs, you silly fool," sighed Mum.

"I knew that! I was just joking around. Lightening the tone." Nobody believed him, but we didn't pursue it.

"Tell us what it means, love," said Mum kindly, not wanting to steal Bethan's thunder.

"These are counterfeit, I'm certain of it. Pretty sloppy work too. The tech bods will take a look at them, but I'm convinced they're fake. This means I was right and someone's been impersonating installers to gain access to people's properties."

"Why would they want to do that? And what's this got to do with the bodies?" I asked.

"Great questions. I'm not sure. But with the boiler suits and now the badges, it's pretty clear that the two things are connected and the two bodies found must be part of it. Definitely the one in the cairn, and I'm suspecting the man you found, too, Max."

"Wait, hang on a mo," said Dad, frowning. "Max filled us in on most of this, but I thought that poor guy in the road was naked. Starkers. What makes you think he's involved in this?"

"Call it a hunch," said Bethan.

"I agree. Otherwise, it's a very big coincidence. Two bodies, they must be connected."

"But why dump him in the middle of the road?" asked Min. "That's just asking for trouble. They could have at least hidden him up here in the cairn like the other guy."

"It's a real head-scratcher, that's for sure," admitted Bethan. "I'm not even meant to be up here again. I got into trouble for it yesterday, and now here we all are. Max, I thought you didn't want to get involved?"

"Me? This isn't my fault. I told everyone what'd been happening and they insisted we come up. But it was a good job we did, right? We found a clue."

"Yes, I suppose this is important. But leave this to the detectives. That goes for all of you."

We mumbled a, "Yes, ma'am," and Bethan nodded seriously. But then she burst into a radiant smile and said, "This is exciting, though, isn't it?"

"You shouldn't be so happy about dead bodies," lectured Mum.

"No, of course not," mumbled Bethan, wilting under Mum's glare.

"But yes, love, it's very exciting. Unless we get murdered." Mum glanced around nervously, as though killers might emerge from behind the wall and do something unspeakable.

"I don't think holidaymakers are a target," said Bethan, putting a hand to Mum's arm to reassure her.

"I hope not."

With the box and contents bagged, we made our way down the hill yet again. At the top of the field Bethan said she'd go and hand everything in and would let me know what the outcome was as soon as she heard something. She admitted that she didn't know when that would be as nobody was falling over themselves to keep her in the loop, but she promised she'd do her best.

With a cuddle from Mum and Dad, much to her surprise, she left.

"Lovely lass," said Dad.

"A real sweetheart," agreed Mum.

"She did seem nice. I can see the attraction," said Min, not meeting my eyes.

"I do not fancy her! She's a kid, or almost. She's just keen to get some real policing done and I happened to be in the right place at the right time."

"Good," grunted Min.

"Good?" I asked, grinning.

"Aw, will you look at these two?" gushed Mum, beaming.

"Now, what's for lunch?" asked Min, changing the subject. "I'm famished."

"Me too," agreed Dad.

"I wasn't expecting any of you. We got supplies for dinner, which you're welcome to have, but as for lunch..."

"Don't you worry about a thing," said Mum proudly.

"Oh no, you didn't?" I asked, groaning.

"Course she did," laughed Dad. "Come on, let's go and get cleaned up then we can eat. I assume they have showers here?"

"Yes, but they're pretty basic."

"As long as it's wet, I don't care. I need to get out of these clothes and I need to wash my hair."

"So do you," Min told me. "You both look like you've been working down the mines."

We returned to Vee and I got towels and shampoo and soap together then Dad and I headed over to the shower block. We took a cubicle each and Dad sang the whole time; a relaxing wash it was not. What he'd been expecting to happen here I didn't know, but he'd still brought a change of clothes and his hair products, so we emerged from the showers looking and smelling fresh and shivering from the cold.

"That was refreshing," he beamed, shaking out like a wet dog on a frosty winter's morning.

"You can say that again!" I laughed. We turned to the sun to warm our faces, basking in the glorious afternoon.

After several seconds, Dad turned serious and asked, "You okay, Son? I know we're the last people you wanted to see, your mum and me anyway, but are you good?"

"I'm fine. Great, in fact. This was the right move for me. I need this. But you didn't have to come."

"You know what your mother's like once she gets an idea in her head. And besides, it wasn't our idea. I told Min it was probably a dodgy signal, but she talked to your mum and it was obvious she was fishing for an excuse to come see you. She misses you, Son. You know that."

"Sometimes I think she wants to get back together, other times I figure I'm just imagining it. We're friends, Dad, that's all. We're divorced."

"I know that, but so what? You think most ex-wives chase down their man the day after he leaves to start a new life without her? Min's just confused. It's been a weird few years for everyone, but we can see the difference in you. Especially with those crimes against footwear. Standards, you have to have standards." Dad scowled at my Crocs.

"They're comfortable. You should try them."

"Never!" he shuddered.

"But you think Min wants to try again? She knows I still love her, and she loves me, but I don't think it's like that. We're just close friends. That's it."

"Just let things play out. She's confused, sure, and that's understandable, but she came, and that's got to count for something."

"Maybe you're right. But I've left, so how would it even work?"

"Would you go back, set up home again?"

"Honestly, I don't know. This is literally day one of my new life and now here you all are. If she asks me to, then I guess I would. But I get the feeling this is my future now. I need to travel. I need to be free. After all that's happened, I need this. Understand?"

"Course I do." Dad slapped me on the back then ruffled my hair like I was still a kid. I laughed despite it.

"Let's go see what Mum's been up to. I can't believe you let her do what I think she's doing."

"You try telling her she can't do something. This is exciting for her. She's nervous too. No matter how old your children get, you still worry. And you've been one helluva worry to us the last few years, so let her have her moment to shine, okay?"

"Sure thing. And I'm sorry about how I was, how I acted. I hardly visited, was always busy, making excuses for being such hard work, and I'm sorry."

"Water under the bridge. You found your way, and that's the main thing. There's more to life than money, and never forget it."

"I won't."

We chatted away as we headed back to the others, smiling and nodding to other guests as we passed. The place was getting busier, with pitches filling up, but there was more than enough room and Dai wasn't precious about how much space people used. I liked places like this, always had, much preferring them to the more corporate holiday parks where everything was there for you, but you didn't have as much freedom and rules were stricter.

I noted that the men who'd tried to press-gang Dai into selling were packing up, at least the goons were. The boss was sitting in the back seat of the Range Rover with the doors open, tapping away on a laptop.

Back at base, it was all go, with Mum and Min busy getting everything ready. Dad winked at me, and I smiled, knowing there was no way to avoid this. Once Mum got an idea in her head, there was no changing her mind, and you either submitted or risked her ire. Mum had lots of ire. She had a recurring monthly Amazon Prime subscription to get a discount and ensure she never ran out.

"It looks incredible," I gushed, knowing it would make Mum proud.

"Thanks. Come on then, let's tuck in. You two look better. Nice and clean."

I stood and surveyed the spread Mum must have spent an absolute fortune on and a lot of time preparing. For special occasions, or trips out, she adored making a hamper. It was an old-fashioned wicker case where the plates, cutlery, even a flask, were included, and she loved to use it. She'd packed just about every kind of cheese, meat, and pickle you could name, and that was just the start. From various other bags she'd produced several artisan loaves, rolls, and not forgetting the tea in the flask. It was obvious where my love of food had come from, and one thing we never went short of when I was young, even if we had little money, was a good meal.

"You really shouldn't have gone to so much trouble," said Min. "It must have cost a bomb."

"It did," grumbled Dad through a mouthful of stuffed olives.

"Nonsense. It wasn't much, and you know I love a hamper."

We spent the next hour eating, laughing, groaning, and tanning ourselves on a perfect day while children played in the field and adults swore at each other quietly about which tent pole went where and who'd forgotten to put the beer in the cool box.

After we'd eaten, then helped clear up, Dad and I did the dishes—this time in bowls on the grass to make life easier and to stay close to everyone. Mum packed everything up and I made fresh tea so we lazed about, laughing at Anxious who half-heartedly kept dropping the ball by someone but couldn't bring himself to chase after it because his belly was so full of food. It would be a light dinner for us both, and my plan for another one-pot wonder was on hold until tomorrow.

"What now?" asked Dad.

"How'd you mean?"

"I mean, about the bodies. Wonder if Bethan's got any information?"

"It was only a few hours ago. I doubt it. And we're best staying out of it, like she said."

"Come on, don't give me that. You must be interested. It's quite an adventure you're having already. I expected you to have got a flat tyre and maybe run out of petrol, or for that old wreck to have just given up the ghost. I didn't expect you to be embroiled in a murder mystery on your first day."

"Thanks for the confidence," I grumbled. "And I'm not embroiled in it. I just happened to find the body."

"Two bodies. And the boiler suits. And now the IDs. You and that young officer are the only ones who have found anything out. Who do you think did it?" he whispered, checking none of the campers were eavesdropping even though there was nobody within earshot.

"How on earth would I know? Sure, there's something fishy going on, obviously, as there are two dead guys, but I don't know who did it."

"Bet Bethan has an opinion," he muttered.

"Maybe you should go and ask her."

"Maybe I will," said Dad in a huff. Everyone stared at him until he relented and admitted, "I won't, and I don't know where she is anyway."

"How about another walk?" suggested Min. "Unless you had other plans? I know we just turned up, but it has been nice. Fun, and certainly interesting. Who would have thought there'd be a crime to solve?"

"A walk sounds great," I agreed. "Shall we take the campervan?"

Everyone was delighted with the idea, so I explained how the doors and seats worked, then Mum and Dad strapped in the back with Anxious, and Min joined me up front. Vee definitely noticed the weight difference as the old engine struggled with the low gear and the hills, but we got going and once on the lanes the ride was if not smooth then at least we were moving forward. My parents commented on the features, even though I'd shown them everything when I bought the camper, and Min asked about the strange handbrake and why was the gear stick so long, so I told her what I knew, which wasn't much, then had an idea.

"Press play on the tape deck," I said, grinning.

"Why, what's on it?"

"You'll see."

With an inquisitive smile, Min pressed play, and the mix tape boomed from the speakers in all its tinny glory.

Summertime by DJ Jazzy Jeff and the Fresh Prince had everyone singing along, laughing and smiling as we coasted along the lanes, the sun dazzling, the air alive with the smells of summer. A veritable cornucopia of eighties and nineties awesomeness was the soundtrack to our mini road trip, and I'll never forget it. Min laughing, Mum wailing, Dad crooning, Anxious howling, and me just grinning, happy to have the people I loved the most in the world with me for the start of my new life. Sure, I'd miss them dearly, but would always go back to visit. That was the beauty of this new home on wheels. I could do whatever I damned well pleased.

We spent the afternoon back on the beach, paddling, throwing the ball for Anxious, and soaking up the sun. Dad even removed his shirt, Mum took off her heels, and Min was down to a bikini without the slightest provocation. She always did love the seaside.

After fish and chips for dinner, as it's almost the law that you have it after a day at the seaside, we drove home weary, happy, full, and covered in sand.

After a cuppa, and with Mum nodding off, Dad said, "Right, we'll be off then." He nudged Mum and she snapped awake.

"I wasn't asleep. I was just resting my eyes."

"And snoring," laughed Dad.

"You were!" she hissed, then took his hand and squeezed.

They sorted out a few things, then Mum kissed me, Dad shook, and they both said, "Look after yourself, and don't get murdered."

"I'll try not to." I turned to Min and asked, "Um, are you good to go? Did you already put your bag in?"

Min glanced from me to my parents, and they both nodded. It seemed words had already been said, and I was the last to know. "I'll stay, if that's alright? I can get the train in the morning."

"Yes, of course! I just assumed..."

"I'd just keep quiet and smile smugly, Son," said Dad with a nod.

"Yes, right."

Soon enough it was just the three of us. Anxious looked from me to Min, barked happily, then took himself off for a nap.

"Don't go getting any ideas," warned Min. "I'm not going to be jumping into bed with you. I know this is confusing for you, Max, it is for me, too, but can we just have a nice evening and not get into anything too deep?"

"Of course. Let's open a bottle of wine, enjoy the view, and have a chat."

"Sounds perfect."

And it was. Right up to bedtime.

Obviously, I offered Min the bed, actually keen to try out the sleeping arrangements up near the roof. I prepared everything well in advance, as per Mickey the seasoned traveller's instructions, and it went smoothly enough. With the roof up, I just had to pull a few boards across above my head and sort out the roll-out mattress.

The only issue was that it cut down the head height in the camper, but as we were outside it wasn't an issue. Bedtime was another matter entirely. With the curtains drawn and everything locked up for the night, Min went coy and undressed under the covers then watched me hopping about on one leg and banging into things as I tried to remove my shorts.

I managed to get up into the "bed" with a little help from the counter, but it was like sliding into a tunnel. I made it eventually, though, and the minute I slid under the covers I had to stifle a groan.

"You need a pee, don't you?"

"No! Who says so?"

"Max, I know you, and I know that you always have a pee once you've got into bed. You should have thought of that."

"Damn, you're right. Now I have to go through all this again. And unlock the camper, and wander around in the dark. I need to fit a bathroom in this thing."

"Good luck with that. Where would it go? Just pee by the hedge. It's dark out."

"Are you allowed? What if everyone did that? The place would stink."

"Max," sighed Min, "everyone does do that. And in case you hadn't noticed, the place does stink."

"Fair enough," I muttered, then went through the whole rigmarole of getting up, unlocking, peeing, locking, banging my head, until, finally, I was back where I started.

"Goodnight, and thank you for a lovely day," said Min dreamily.

"You are more than welcome. Thanks for coming. It was a real treat."

I woke in the morning to find Min gone and a letter on the bed.

Sorry, it's too much. This was a bad idea. I do love you though. Min.

Deflated, and a little surprised, I dressed rapidly, let Anxious out for a pee, had one myself, then dove back into the camper and drove after her. It was miles to the station, and anything might happen to her. Had she forgotten that there was a murderer on the loose?

Chapter 13

There was no sign of Min on the lanes, and I wondered if she'd managed to call a taxi, or hitch a ride, or if something awful had happened. What if she'd been picked up by the killer and was lying dead in the road or stuffed into a cairn never to be found until the badgers had eaten her face off?

I was beginning to freak out.

Checking my phone repeatedly, and I knew I shouldn't whilst driving but this was too important to abide by the rules, I whooped when I got a signal then pulled over and called her.

"Are you okay?"

"Yes, fine. I'm at the station. I had a signal so booked a taxi. What's wrong? You sound weird."

"Oh, wow. Great. Not great you left, but great you aren't hurt. Min, I was worried. I kept thinking something bad might have happened."

"Sorry, I didn't think. Max, everything is fine, but I need some space. We'll talk in a few days. I'm sorry to mess you around like this, I truly am. I don't know what I'm doing, and I'm being very foolish. Forgive me?"

"Of course I do."

"Thanks. Bye."

So that was the end of that. I shouldn't have got my hopes up, but Min was right and she should never have come. It just made things harder for the both of us.

I drove home in silence, not in the mood for music.

Anxious kept sniffing the seat, then searching the van. He looked at me with his doleful eyes and whined.

"I know, buddy. I miss her too. But it's just us guys, and we need to accept that."

Anxious lay down and curled up with a groan of resignation. I felt like doing the same.

Back at the campsite, I did the usual and opened the gate then closed it behind me once I'd driven through and parked off to the side.

Bethan and another woman were there talking to Dai. Bethan was in tears, Dai was clearly in a huff, and the woman was clearly angry too.

"...told you, I'm not doing it!" growled Dai.

"They won't leave us alone, you know that. Dad, it's a bloody fortune. You could do anything, go anywhere. And what about me and Bethan, eh? What about us? You know my Hywel can't find enough work. It's hard on us. Bethan's got her own career now, but oh no, you're being as stubborn as always."

"You think what you want," grumbled Dai, then turned his back on her.

"I give up!" The woman stormed off over to her car.

Bethan spoke quietly to Dai and he nodded then returned to the house. The door slammed shut behind him.

Being the nosy sod I was, and with the rather opportune fact that Anxious had raced over to say hello, I wandered over to Bethan.

"We have to stop meeting like this."

"Bethan, I'm leaving," called the woman, arms crossed, frowning. She looked just like an older version of Bethan. Mid-fifties, with the same cute cheeks and squat but slim figure, but whereas Bethan was smart in her uniform, her mother was in dirty jeans and green wellies with a check shirt over a dark vest. Clearly a farmer, just like her father.

"You go on, I have things to do," she called.

"Shall I get the gate for her?"

"Don't bother. She'll be back over in a heartbeat, you just wait."

"She your mum?"

"How did you guess?"

"Just a hunch," I laughed.

Her mum did come over, arms still folded, and she hardly paid me any attention beyond a quick glance, then asked, "Well, what did he say? You have to make him see sense."

"Mum, he doesn't want to sell. You have to accept that."

"Is Dai getting grief from those guys again? The Happy Valleys goons?" I asked.

The woman turned on me and hissed, "Who are you? What do you know about it?"

"Mum, this is Max. Max, this is Gwen, my mum."

"Nice to meet you." I put out my hand to shake and she took it quickly then ignored me.

"Talk to your taid. Make him see sense, the old fool."

"Taid?" I asked.

"It's Welsh for grandad," explained Bethan.

"Our first language," hissed Gwen, her strong accent making it clear she disapproved of me being English. "And who the bloody hell are you? Why are you here?"

"I'm staying here."

"He's the guy I told you about. The one who found the body in the road and helped with things up at the cottage."

"Ah, you're the one getting my daughter into trouble."

"What?"

"Mum! Stop it, you're embarrassing me."

"Just try to convince your taid. This has gone on long enough. We could be rich and taking it easy instead of me and your dad having to work all the hours. Whoever thought I'd be a farmer at my age?"

"Dad loves it, and so do you."

"Maybe, but that's not the point. It doesn't put bread on the table. Not anymore. I'm off. See you later."

"I'll get the gate for you."

Gwen grunted, but I did the gentlemanly thing and opened and closed the gate after her.

Bethan joined me and bent to fuss over Anxious whose ears were down. "It's alright, there's no more shouting now the nasty lady has gone."

Anxious wagged and was soon back to his jovial self. He hated arguments and raised voices, wanting everyone to get along and be happy. Didn't we all?

"More trouble?" I asked.

"You could say that. It's been going on for years. Grandad has always said he'd leave the campsite to me. Mum and Dad have the farm side of things and for years they were happy with that. But farming is so hard now, there's no money in it, and they want out."

"Can't they help around here?"

"There's not enough to do. And Grandad likes to stay active. Mum and Dad help out sometimes, but it's not a full-time wage."

"But this will be yours, not theirs?"

"Yeah, it's an issue. But Grandad insisted. He wants to ensure I have a steady income. He said my parents could run it once he retires, which I think will be soon, but they aren't pleased about it."

"It is unusual. Normally, people leave things to their children. He's your mum's dad?"

"Yes, but they have a rocky history. Mum's never been very good with money, and Dad's never been able to rein her in. She always wants more, is never satisfied. He can't get a full-time position away from here even though he tries so hard, so just helps out with the sheep and the other ventures they have going on, but it's not his thing. He isn't a farmer. Grandad wants me to have the place. I'm here more than at home anyway, and have always stayed with him a few nights a week. We don't all get on, in case you hadn't noticed."

"I might have had my suspicions," I chortled. "Sorry, that must be hard."

"No, it's fine. But now there's this company wanting to buy the place and Mum and Dad want Dai to sell. It's millions. We could be set up for life. But Grandad won't hear of it. He said it's family land and he wants it to stay that way. That's the reason he won't leave it to my folks. Mum would sell it straight away. He even said he would leave it to them if they agreed to a clause that meant they would never sell. Mum refused."

"But you wouldn't sell?"

"Never. This is my home, always has been. We lived here for years with Taid, then we got our own place. It's just a basic house and in town, but this is where my heart is. I'm going to move back up here with Grandad in a few weeks, as I need the space. Mum and Dad won't let this lie."

"So they're pestering Dai to sell?"

"Yes, especially now after those idiots came and gave him grief yesterday. Mum heard about it and says he's a fool for not taking the money. She's also tried to convince him it isn't safe. With the bodies piling up, she told him the place is going under anyway. Reckons nobody will want to come once the word gets out that people have been murdered here. I have to admit, it's not good for business."

"It must be tempting to sell up."

"Some things are worth more than money."

"True, and you're right."

"Look at this place. Everyone has space, they're happy, the views are incredible, and it's just so special. Grandad wants to spend whatever years he has left here, and I don't blame him."

We stared off at the sea, the sun still shining down on the beauty all around us.

"Neither do I."

"But that's enough about me and my problems. What about you? Was that really your ex and your parents? They didn't leave you alone for long."

"No, they didn't, but it was a nice surprise. Min left this morning."

"Oh, you lucky sod," said Bethan with a sly wink.

"It wasn't like that. I slept in the weird bed up by the roof. But she left early, said it was a mistake."

"Oh, I'm sorry. But she must care to have come to check on you."

"She does, but it's complicated."

"That's life for you."

"You, Bethan, are a very wise young woman. Any news on the case?"

"Not a lot. The detectives are still put out that I'd found more clues. They might want to talk to you again, but maybe not. They're looking into it, but so far nothing. But the day is young, so who knows what will happen?"

"Let's wait and see. I hope you figure it out. You going to keep investigating?"

"Actually, yes. I'm off to find the last few installers. That's my job for the day. Ask a few questions. They're letting me be more involved now I keep finding leads for them."

"Hey, that's great!"

"Cool, eh?" beamed Bethan. "If I could solve the case, I'd get some proper policing to do."

"Then go get 'em," I laughed.

"I will. I just came to check on things with Mum and make sure Grandad was alright, but let's hope the day brings some insight into this nasty business."

"Let's hope so. See you soon."

Anxious pawed at Bethan's leg as she went to leave, so she bent and gave him a fuss until he was satisfied, then he hopped into the van and we returned to our spot.

I'd left the chairs and bits and pieces out as the one problem with moving your accommodation was that someone could take your pitch. I needed a better system, as if it was raining I'd want to keep everything dry. Time to get one of those shelters that almost every other camper seemed to have. The days of simple tents were long gone now, it seemed. Families brought everything bar the kitchen sink, and sometimes that too, with huge tents with porches and either gazebos or open-sided shelters. Some even had ones with insect netting. I needed to up my camping game, and a shelter did seem like a good idea so I could be out in all weathers rather than having to retreat to the van if it rained.

First, breakfast, and a cup of well-deserved coffee. I busied myself sorting things out and wondering about Min. Why had she come? Why leave so suddenly? I just didn't understand. It was out of character and irrational, but maybe that was the point? She wanted to be free like me, and this was her way of testing the waters, so to speak? Did she want us to get back together? She knew I did. Time would tell, and I knew better than to pester her. I'd wait to hear from her, or call her in a few days or a week once she'd had time to figure things out.

Time to put myself first anyway. I couldn't spend my life stuck in a what-if quandary. There was nothing I could do about Min's state of mind, and I knew her well enough to know any attempt to interfere would be futile.

A fry-up done outside on the portable cooker sorted me out, and saved getting grease in the VW. Another problem I would have to contend with and made a mental note to get some decent cleaning products. Just more on an increasing list of things I needed to buy to make my home more manageable. Where was it all going to fit? The campervan wasn't exactly massive, but others must manage so I would too.

After cleaning up and meticulously storing everything, I checked around and optimised belongings in any way I could. Opening the back and arranging things there gave me a surprising amount of room, so I spent some time going through everything, utilising space as efficiently as possible, then grunted in satisfaction at a job well done.

"Time for a bit of shopping, Anxious," I called to my sleepy dog, curled up on the bench seat and snoring happily.

He opened a lazy eye, yawned, then stretched out before moving to the passenger seat and curling up again.

"Feeling worn out, eh?" I chuckled, realising I was exhausted too after a fitful night's sleep and the madness that seemed to be following us around since we began our new life.

Driving into Rhyl town, I went over recent events, trying to make some sense of them, wondering if there was a link between the seemingly disparate events. The bodies, one wrapped in a tent, the other in the cairn, the boiler suits, the IDs, e-energy, even the strange man, Barry Simms, seemingly watching me, and the Happy Valley Corporation with their heavy-handed tactics for trying to get Dai to sell his farm and give up his way of life.

Could the company be killing people to make the place go out of business then snap it up for a bargain? Would they go that far? But why the e-energy angle? How did that tie in? Why the body in the cairn?

"Damn, how do detectives figure this stuff out?" I muttered to myself.

Anxious stared at me blankly, having no insights.

"Maybe we need to approach this from a different angle?" I mused. "But since when was I even looking into this?" It was then that I realised that I wanted to figure out this terrible crime. I liked Dai, sort of, but what about Bethan? If this didn't get solved, it would put a real dent in the reviews for the campsite and could well lead to it closing entirely.

People weren't going to pick a location where bodies kept appearing in the road. Once word got out, and I bet it had already, bookings would plummet and the site might never recover. Bethan would be inheriting a business with no income and no future, and she didn't deserve that at all.

"What can we do, Anxious?" I asked my tired pooch as I spied a parking spot on a busy section of road as a car pulled out right in front of me.

Anxious whined and pawed at the window to let me know, so I indicated, pulled alongside the other vehicles, then began reversing.

Reversing! I hadn't practised like I said I would, and wasn't used to the size of the campervan. Would I even fit? I needed to pay attention to these things. Using the mirrors, and as much luck as judgement, I managed to squeeze into the space with a rather smug smile for a job well done, and only then did I surreptitiously wipe the sweat from my brow, more from the stress than the heat of the morning.

It promised to be a real scorcher, so I figured I'd leave the vents open on the windows as no way could anyone squeeze inside.

With Anxious on the lead because the place was rammed with shoppers, and I didn't want to risk him getting lost, I headed to the right, but Anxious whined and tugged at the lead.

"You want to go the other way?"

Anxious tugged harder, his whining more insistent, so I shrugged and let him pick the direction. I had no idea what shops were where, so it didn't matter and it wasn't like we were up against the clock anyway. I smiled at the thought. I had all the time in the world.

We'd only gone past a few shops when Anxious dragged me into the doorway of a women's clothes store then sat, eyes focused on something several shops down. He turned to me and looked into my eyes, then whined again before locking back on whatever had taken his interest.

"What have you seen?" I asked, knowing Anxious had excellent vision and an even better sense of smell. He was an expert at tracking, always sniffing out whatever he was chasing, not that he ever caught anything, but I didn't remind him of such things as he was a sensitive soul.

His nostrils were opening and closing rapidly as he snorted in the scents, eyes never leaving his mark.

"Is that Bethan's mum? Who's that with her? And who else is there?"

I ducked back further into the shade and shelter of the doorway, my eyes now as focused on them as Anxious'. If he wanted to spy on Gwen, then there was a very good reason.

Or maybe he just didn't like her attitude and wanted to wait until she moved on before we went about our business? I wasn't exactly keen to meet her again, that was for sure. I crouched and stroked his head as he watched intently.

Gwen, and I assumed it was her husband Hywel with her, were talking to what appeared to be a homeless man. He was sitting on the ground, nothing but a sheet of cardboard between him and the dirty pavement, with several bags by his side. The husband pulled out a wallet as they spoke and gave the man a note. The grizzled looking guy was clearly grateful, and then more notes were wafted in front of him and both Gwen and her husband began talking at once as Gwen pointed to a grubby white van parked opposite.

The homeless man indicated his things, but Hywel shrugged then they exchanged a few more words before the man nodded and Gwen crossed the road while Hywel helped the bewildered man stand. Hywel grabbed the bags and the destitute man followed him across the road then waited while Gwen slid open the side door. He got in, the man's things were carefully loaded, then the door slammed closed.

Hywel and Gwen checked around them then both got in the front and drove off.

"That was weird," I noted. "Well done for spotting them."

Anxious wagged happily as he turned and smiled at me. He lifted a paw, so we shook, then had to move when the shop owner opened the door and scowled at us.

"Time for some shopping. I wonder what they were doing with that guy? Giving him somewhere to stay, some food, or maybe they get desperate guys to help out on the farm? I bet it's a cheap source of labour."

Something didn't feel right about it at all, so I did a sudden about turn and hurried back to the campervan.

"We need to follow them," I told Anxious as I fastened his seatbelt. "Don't ask me why, but this feels wrong. Very wrong."

Anxious nodded in agreement, attention focused on the white van several cars in front as it headed out of town.

Chapter 14

The mud-splattered Ford Transit raced through the streets of Rhyl then back the way I'd just come, heading towards the farm. Hywel was clearly used to the lanes because he hardly slowed even on tight bends, missing the high stone walls or burgeoning hedges by millimetres. Then he'd suddenly slam on the brakes just when needed to navigate a seemingly impossible turn only to race off ahead.

The ancient Volkswagen had a hard time keeping up, and I'd never changed gears so much in such a short time in my life, but I kept them in my sights and thankfully the lanes were quiet. We only had to pull in at two passing spots where luck was on our side rather than having to try to reverse around blind bends.

Approaching the Golygfa Maes farm and campsite, the Transit took a right turn heading up and around the hill. The going was rough, with the road terribly pot-holed and the hedges overgrown, so Anxious and I clenched our buttocks, grimaced at the jolts up our spines, and I considered investing in better suspension. Over a cattle grid, through an open gate, then before I knew it we were in a large, steeply sloping field with a series of large polytunnels up ahead where the ground levelled out at the top of the rise.

It was so sudden that I didn't have time to consider what to do, and before I could think I was forced to stop as the Transit came to a halt in front of the polytunnels and the engine was turned off.

I pulled on the handbrake then let the engine stutter into silence. Scenarios played out in my mind regards what I could say. This could get very weird, very fast. I decided a simple lost tourist act would be the best option, saying I was following them as I thought they were going to the campsite.

A man emerged from the first polytunnel and opened the door to let Hywel out and they began talking. Hywel nodded, then joined Gwen on the other side and helped the homeless man out of the back. Two others exited after him; I hadn't even known they were inside.

Gwen caught sight of me, so I reluctantly got out and wandered over with Anxious close by my heels. She scowled at me as her husband had a quick word with the men then stood by her side and whispered in her ear. Neither took their eyes off me the entire time.

I glanced to my right at the men being spoken to by the one who'd greeted Hywel and Gwen, giving them instructions on how to pick strawberries. Then things clicked into place and I calmed. This was a business, and a potentially lucrative one, but in recent years it had become increasingly difficult to get people willing to do the work that either wasn't well-paid enough or easy enough for anyone to be interested. I'd heard stories of whole harvests going to ruin because producers couldn't get enough pickers.

"Hi," I said, waving and smiling as I approached.

Gwen put her hands on her hips and scowled, her eyes narrowing, while her husband merely watched through a mop of curly brown hair, his black vest stained and in desperate need of a wash. The man, maybe a manager, who had given the new arrivals instructions, paused, said a few more words to them, then pointed inside and said he'd be with them soon.

"What are you doing here?" asked Gwen.

"Who is this?" asked Hywel.

"Hywel, this is the man who Bethan keeps talking about. The one who found the body in the road and was with her when she found the one at the cottage."

"And the boiler suits, and now ID tags too," I said, still smiling. "Hi, I'm Max."

"Hywel," said Hywel, shaking hands with me. His fingers were stained red, the palms calloused, and the grip was overly tight.

"Nice to meet you. You should be proud, both of you. Your daughter is a fine woman and has been very kind to me. She's a credit to you both, and I'm sure she's got a great future ahead of her."

"At least someone has," grunted Gwen.

"No need to be sour. Max was just being friendly, right?" said Hywel brightly, a warm smile spreading when I praised his daughter.

He wasn't what I'd expected, and seemed jovial and friendly whereas his wife was the opposite. He was a wiry man, with a dark tan and laughter lines around his eyes. He also looked tired, like someone who had the weight of the world on his shoulders but still refused to give in or let it sour his underlying personality. I liked Hywel.

"Absolutely."

"And Bethan speaks very highly of you. Poor girl has been having a hard time finding her place in the force. They don't take too kindly to pretty young woman wanting the best cases. She's learning, and it will settle down, but that girl wants to be a detective inspector before she's even nabbed her first criminal," laughed Hywel.

"The optimism of youth. I don't doubt she'll be one of the youngest detectives they've ever had. She seems to have a real talent for police work."

"Hey, you aren't too shabby yourself finding all these clues."

"More accident than skill," I admitted.

"What can we do for you, Max?" asked Gwen, scowling.

"Oh, nothing. I got a little lost. Wasn't paying attention. When I saw the van, I hoped it was going to the campsite so just followed along behind. Seems I got that wrong."

"You sure did," chuckled Hywel. "Take a right once you get back down the hill. If you'd just kept on going straight you would have found it."

"I figured that once I didn't recognise anything, but there was nowhere to turn around. So, strawberries is it? I'm assuming that's what I can smell?"

Anxious trotted over to Hywel and began licking his jeans where he'd clearly rubbed his hands on them.

"Yeah," Hywel scratched his head, "but it's another idea that hasn't really panned out too well. We keep trying different things to keep the money coming in, but running a farm and making a living don't seem like a good combination. I get other work when I can, but this isn't the big city and everyone's in the same boat."

"What we need is for Dad to see sense and sell the whole lot," grumbled Gwen.

"Hey, we've been over this," said Hywel with a sympathetic hand to her shoulder. "It's his whole life. This place is in his blood.

Yours too. And Bethan's. If he doesn't want to sell, then that's up to him. At least we know Bethan will be taken care of."

"Yes, but what about us?"

"We get by. Now, I'm sure Max doesn't want to hear about our finances. You want a job, Max? Want to pick strawberries for the day? It's minimum wage, but you can eat as many as you want."

"Um, no thanks, but it's a tempting offer. You got enough staff?"

"Nowhere near," admitted Hywel. "We've resorted to scouring the town for anyone who's hard up and willing to come put in a day's work. It's a crying shame. Nobody wants the work."

"Well, good luck, and I hope you manage to pick them on time."

"Oh we will." Hywel rubbed his hands together. "We have no choice if we want to make at least a small profit from the harvest. They need picking every day, so we work whatever hours are needed to ensure we get every juicy one of them. We're here every morning at the crack of dawn."

"Sorry, and you are?" I asked politely, turning my attention on the stoic man yet to speak who'd wandered over mid-conversation.

"Oh, right, should have made introductions," said Hywel, looking uncomfortable for not making them earlier. "Very bad manners of me." Gwen tutted, but he frowned at her then smiled and said, "This is Bernard. He's invaluable around here. He helped set up this whole operation a few years back. He's the farm manager and does more work than anyone. Strawberries are his speciality, though, and he does an amazing job."

I put out a hand and shook his surprisingly soft but very large hand. I noted the deep red, almost purple stains covering his hands. It was much more ingrained than on Hywel's or Gwen's.

"Nice to meet you."

"Likewise," I said. "Guess that's from picking all the strawberries?" I asked, pointing to his hands.

He looked down at them then back to me. "Yes, the staining never comes off. It takes weeks after the harvest has finished. We do blueberries, too, and they're even worse."

"I bet," I laughed. "So, you manage the whole place, eh?"

"Someone has to," muttered Gwen with a scowl for Hywel.

"Not this again. I told you, if I've got other work I can't be in two places at once. And this is your thing, not mine."

"It's meant to be our thing," hissed Gwen with a quick glance at me, clearly not wanting to get into this too deeply with me there.

"What my wife is so sweetly trying to say, is that we need Bernard to run things because we can't handle it all ourselves. I'm often off doing other work if I can find it, even filling in for people at e-energy if they're off sick. I used to be an electrician, but those days seem to unfortunately be long gone."

"Why'd you pack it in?"

"Just couldn't get the work after the big companies moved in. I tried with e-energy for a while but it didn't work with the farm. Like I said, can't be in two places at once. But hopefully they'll take me back on full-time at some point. We need them to. But Bernard here is a real help. He focuses on things up here, but it's like he's split down the middle sometimes when it gets busy. He's everywhere at the same time."

"Sounds like you're holding it all together," I said, smiling.

"I try my best. And Hywel is too kind. He works just as hard as me." This caused Gwen to grunt, but both men ignored her. Seemed they were used to it. "But I was born to this life, Hywel not so much."

"I'm more of a townie," he explained. "But I love it here and wouldn't change it for the world now. All this fresh air, the hard work, the views. It's incredible, right?"

"Stunning," I agreed. "I'm jealous. Well, it looks like you have a great set-up, and I'll be sure to buy some produce before I leave. You have it outside the farmhouse, right?"

"Yes, there's always something for sale. Just see Dai about it, or leave the money in the honesty box," said Hywel.

"I will. See you around," I said, then nodded to them and retreated with Anxious to the van.

I watched the odd couple follow Bernard and enter the polytunnel where they would no doubt work late until they'd finished the harvest. It really was a hard life, and I didn't envy them, but Gwen sure was down on her father. Children shouldn't resent their parents for wanting a life of their own. Surely everyone had to make their own way in the world to some degree?

I was just glad that nothing untoward was happening. For a while there, I'd got carried away and wondered if they were doing something unspeakable with the man they picked up from town, but they were just looking for some help. Not to dress him up in an e-energy uniform, give him a fake ID then kill him. I was definitely getting carried away with things. But it did give me an idea.

Could whoever the dead men were be related to simple thefts? Were there a string of unsolved burglaries in the area and that's what the whole affair was about? I'd have to ask Bethan when I saw her, although I assumed the police would have already been looking into that. There must be a reason for the IDs. That was most likely it, but why were they dead? Or could there be another reason why they were impersonating smart meter installers?

What could that be?

And why dump the man in the road outside the campsite? It was too sloppy, and just didn't add up.

With the morning shopping interrupted by what ended up being a wild goose chase, I headed back down the lane for the third time and vowed it would be my last for the day. This was not the relaxing start I'd envisioned, what with everyone arriving yesterday and the madness that preceded it, but I took it with good humour and a positive outlook as there were bound to be issues when embarking on such a life, right? Maybe not murderous, but in its own way it was exciting, if rather worrying if I dwelt on the darker side of such things.

Lucking out with a parking spot on the edge of town, Anxious and I took our time wandering the high street, enjoying the weather, inspecting various shops, and generally acting like tourists but with a keen eye out for cleaning products and cheap plastic bowls.

For lunch, I got a simple pasta dish from a deli that was surprisingly good, but I needed to get better at preparing all my meals as money could soon run out if I didn't live within my modest monthly budget. It wasn't a poor man's budget, but neither was I made of cash, and buying meals, and certainly coffees, would have to be limited because it all added up.

Every time we spied a police officer, Anxious would tug on his lead, keen to go and say hello because he thought it was Bethan. Only when we got closer did he realise it wasn't her, the lead suddenly going slack as he lost interest. Was it normal to have such a large police presence in such a small town, or was this why it was seen as such a safe place to live?

He spied another uniform halfway down the high street and this time he wasn't taking no for an answer. With an almighty surge, he almost dislocated my shoulder, no mean feat for such a little dude, and I had to race to get some slack before he either choked or I lost the lead.

"Cool it, Anxious, you nearly had my arm off." I pulled back gently and he eased up, eyes locked on the officer's back, nose working overtime.

He whined, and his tail was stiff. Anxious had found his mark.

"Fine, it's her, so play it cool. You want a fuss, don't you?" Anxious barked that he did, tail now wagging.

"Then be cool as a cucumber. You have to relax, not look so eager. You'll get your fuss soon enough."

Taking my words to mean tug really hard and begin yapping away like a loon, we trotted over to the startled Bethan as she turned to see what the noise was.

She smiled as she spied us, then called for Anxious who leaped into her arms as I released his lead and began licking her face, tail spinning so fast I heard the slap as it thumped against her starched uniform.

"Constable Bethan Jones, we meet again," I grinned. "Sorry about Anxious, but he really likes you and wasn't about to play it cool like I told him to."

"That's okay," she laughed, moving him from her face and tickling his tummy so he'd stop wriggling so much. "Did you miss me?"

"Um, a little," I said, thinking it was a strange thing to ask.

Bethan frowned, then chuckled heartily as she said, "I was talking to Anxious."

"Um, of course, and I was just pretending to answer for him," I stammered, the words sounding lame even to me.

"Liar!" she said, bending to let Anxious down who rubbed against her leg and then sat and looked up expectantly.

"I think he wants to go for a W word."

"A W word? A widdle?"

"No, you know, when you put one leg in front of the other."

"A walk?"

"No, don't say it!" But it was too late, and although Anxious was already on a walk, he began doing laps around us both and barking excitedly.

"Sorry, I didn't mean to do that," Bethan giggled.

"I think you did. I think you want a break and you want to show us where the best park is around here."

"I could do with a rest. It's been an exhausting day. I've spoken to installers, been into people's houses, even some businesses, trying to uncover anything untoward but nobody has anything bad to say about e-energy and nobody has heard anything about people going missing. It's a real head-scratcher."

"What about them reporting things stolen? Could a gang be using fake IDs to gain access to people's homes then rob them like you thought?"

"I was sure that would be it, but it doesn't seem that way. Nobody's reported anything, and everyone said the installers were professional and knew what they were doing, and were fast too. They even took their boots off. That's some well-trained workers."

"Sounds like it. So a dead end then?"

"Seems that way. Here, let's cross the road and I'll show you the park."

We made slow progress as people stopped to chat with Bethan. She was clearly well-known in the town and everyone greeted her with a kindly smile, or almost everyone. There were a few who were less enthusiastic, and some who were either abrupt or blanked her entirely, and when it happened again I raised an eyebrow.

"Don't worry about it. You get used to it. Most people like knowing their streets are safe and the police are looking out for them, but there are always those who think we're the bad ones and they don't trust us. It doesn't help that I'm young and..."

"Pretty?"

"I didn't want to say it, but yes. I know I don't look too bad, and honestly it doesn't help. They don't take me seriously and yet they still dislike me because they think I'm a traitor. As though being on the side of the law is a bad thing."

"Ignore them. Once you find the killer, or killers, you'll be the local hero."

"I wish I could. It would be awesome," she beamed, her cute dimples showing her eagerness to solve the crime.

"Maybe you will. There must be something to go on, surely? Any news from the coroner?"

"Yes, actually, there is. It's very strange."

"Really? I like strange. Do tell."

"You like strange?"

"Sorry, I don't know why I said that. What I meant to say is that I'm getting over-excited by this intrigue and I'm keen to hear what the latest is. As long as you're allowed to tell me?"

"Not really, no. So you didn't hear it from me, okay, Max?"

"You have my word. And Anxious promises to keep quiet too."

Anxious barked, causing us both to laugh.

"Here's the park, Rhyl's finest. Let's let Anxious have a run around and we can get a coffee from the kiosk. It's pretty good, actually."

"Sounds perfect."

With Anxious busy marking his new territory, sniffing bums, and barking up trees at taunting squirrels, I got our coffees then joined Bethan on a bench. She removed her hat, ran her fingers through her hair to loosen it out, then sighed as she took a sip.

"Ah, that's nice. Should have got a lolly though. It's a bit warm for coffee."

"Hot drinks are best when it's warm. It cools you down."

"I've always heard that, but I don't buy it."

"It's true. If you have something cold, your body warms up to get you back to temperature. But if you have something hot, your body actually cools down to return you to baseline. It works, honest."

"If you say so, but it's good either way."

We drank in silence for a while, watching the people in the park, then I turned to Bethan and asked, "What about the tent? Has that been looked into? Maybe it was bought around here and the shop owner will remember the man."

"Already done, and no go. Nobody remembers, or it was bought somewhere else."

"Oh, that's a shame. So, what did the coroner say?"

"The man in the tent broke his neck, but not before he suffocated. Or almost suffocated. From what I was told, it seems there were things that made it seem like he had trouble breathing, but that it was a fall that most likely killed him."

"How long had he been dead for when I found him?"

"A few hours, less than twelve. It was a fresh corpse, so to speak."

"But no other marks on him?"

"Nothing beyond what you'd expect when you fall off a vehicle. Which means he was most likely just shoved out the back of a van or something. He might still have been alive, but landed badly and broke his neck and that was the end of the guy."

"Why was he naked though?"

"We have no idea. The obvious answer is so that nobody could identify him or trace evidence from his clothes. But it might be for another reason."

"Care to share?"

"It's just a theory, but what if he had been wearing one of the boiler suits and took it off then maybe removed the rest of his clothes, too, and burned them? It would explain the fire, then the suit up the chimney."

"But why do that? And then what? Walk down the hill naked, get wrapped in a tent? That doesn't sound right."

"If he was with someone else it would. He stripped to get rid of the evidence, then the other person killed him and hid the suit because they didn't want to risk the fire being seen. Or they got into a fight. I honestly don't know, and we just aren't finding anything out."

"You'll work it out, I'm sure. What about the body in the cairn?"

"Total dead end. Nothing to report beyond that the corpse was old. At least six months, maybe more. With no idea who it was."

"But they have to be related, right?"

"I think so, but not everyone does. It might just be one of those crazy coincidences."

"But it's doubtful."

"Yes, it is."

We drank the rest of our coffee in silence. Then it was time for Bethan to get back to work. With an excited farewell from Anxious and a less tongue-based goodbye from me, we watched her go then remained in the park until Anxious was empty of bladder and ready to hit the shops once more.

Chapter 15

By mid-afternoon we were done with shopping and certainly done with the heat. Trying to control an excited dog whilst holding onto various household goods was a sure way to induce heatstroke. The place was rammed, and we'd both had enough. As we emerged from the final shop, I spied an e-energy van straddling the pavement where the driver had squeezed into a tight spot and decided to have a word.

"Excuse me," I said brightly to the man closing the van door and lugging a large black case to the ground.

"Yes, mate, what can I do for you?" he asked, shaking out his hands to get the feeling back.

"Sorry to bother you, and I know you might find this weird, but I was wondering if I could have a word and ask if any of the other installers have gone missing?"

"Missing? You mean like off on the sick?" he frowned, scratching at his shaved head.

"No, I mean like left suddenly and never come back?"

"Mate, this is a sweet gig. You'd have to be nuts to do that."

"So nobody you can't account for?"

"Not a single one. I wouldn't know about other places. Ah, I get it. This is about the murders, right? I spoke to a hot young police chick about it, and she wanted to know the same."

"Yes, I think I might know her. So, you heard about the murders?"

"Everyone around here did. Didn't take a genius to work out what she was getting at, even though she didn't say as much. Nice woman. Bit too pretty to be a police officer though. You need larger birds with meaty arms and a face like a baby's slapped bum to put the fear of God into the late-night drunken louts around here."

"You get a lot of trouble in town sometimes, do you?"

"Honestly, mate, no, we don't. Lived here my whole life, and I guess I'm one of the drunken idiots come Friday, but no, everyone's cool. It's a quiet town where everyone knows everyone. I know Bethan, we went to school together actually. She's a good cop, but like I said, too pretty to scare people."

"I understand. Anything funny been going on then? Anything at all?"

"Like what?"

"I don't know," I admitted. "Just something different with work, or places you've been? People acting out of character, that sort of thing?"

"Mate, again, Bethan asked me all that."

"Okay, then how about this? What would you tell a guy and his dog who's being nosy and can't get this out of his mind because he found both corpses, that you wouldn't tell the police, no matter how cute they are and how well you know them?"

The installer, Ian, going by his ID, checked the street then pulled me close to the van. "This is strictly between us, right, and I swear if this ever comes back to me then I will hunt you down and you'll be the third corpse found. You get me?"

"I get you. I swear your name won't ever be mentioned."

Ian looked down at his ID and flipped it over so I couldn't see, then sighed. "This is serious, man, and I don't know if I should tell."

"I think you should. It's obviously worrying you. Look, I'm just trying to get this over with. I keep finding bodies and I'm worried for everyone's safety. Can't you help me out here? Help everyone out. Are you at risk? In danger?"

"No, at least I don't think so, but here's the deal. Sometimes, and I don't mean often, right, we might do a bit of a favour for someone."

"A favour?"

"Yeah, you know, maybe hook them up with a few things that aren't strictly a hundred percent legal. Now, I'm not saying I've ever done such a thing, but if had, it might have been a rather strange night."

"Night, how'd you mean? You work at night?"

"Not officially, no. It's strictly smart meter installs currently for this job, but I'm an electrician and I used to just do anything that came my way. Meters, rewiring, running new cables for ovens or showers, whatever."

"I get you. So what happened? Or might have happened that you heard about?" I said, winking.

"If someone were to have taken a backhander for helping set up cheap power and electric heating for the parents of a very pretty police officer, they wouldn't be about to tell her that, now would they?"

"I don't suppose they would, no."

"Especially if it would mean he would definitely lose his job and maybe even face a conviction, no matter that it paid very well."

"I get it, and, of course, I would never know who might have done such a thing."

"No, course you wouldn't," he grunted, nodding knowingly. "And if the people who paid this mystery installer to ensure their undercover crops grew well despite bad weather early in the season refused to heed the installers insistence on certain safety measures and they ended up getting repeat electric shocks which might be fatal, then he'd have no choice but to cut them off, now wouldn't he?"

"He wouldn't have any choice, no. Nobody would want to risk anyone dying."

"Exactly. So the installer cut them off, but if they rewired it themselves to use someone else's power supply and bypass the bills, then the installer would be in a bit of a quandary, wouldn't he?"

"He really would. But he might not want to get involved now because of what he'd done before."

"Exactly."

"Okay, so what are you saying? There was an accident?"

"Yes, mate, there was. Some poor homeless dude got the shock of his life because Bethan's folks messed with my install. They called me up and I went to take a look and they'd screwed around by running more wires and taking more energy from Dai. I went spare, disconnected the lot, and told them they better not touch it. But they have, and I'm not happy. It's only a matter of time before they get someone killed, and it's stressing me out. I'm going to go back up and cut them off again, but Dai's a right handful and a wily old bugger, so it's risky, but he's nothing compared to his daughter. A pussycat in comparison. Gwen's ferocious."

"But the guy was okay? He lived?"

"Sure, but he was burned and really shaken up."

"Do you think it had anything to do with the murders?"

"The murders? No, how could it?" Ian thought for a moment, then the light bulb in his head clicked on.

"Damn, I hadn't thought of that. I was just telling you what had been weird around here lately and how they might end up hurting someone. But yeah, maybe they pushed it too far and someone did die. What now?"

"Don't worry. The man they found didn't have any burns from electricity, and so it couldn't have been them."

"That's a relief. But look, my name is not to be mentioned. Understand?"

"I do. And thanks. It's something to think about, and it certainly shows how little Gwen thinks of her dad."

"She's always been a handful, but Dai's a great bloke. He's hilarious. Scary too. I never know if he's messing around or not."

"Thanks again. And no more dodgy installs?"

"Mate, I hear you. After that I'm strictly by the book. Take it easy." He lugged his gear over to the shop and entered.

What did all that mean? Did it mean anything? Did it have a bearing on this? What should I do next?

"Time to go home, Anxious. We need to put our feet up and start relaxing."

And boy did we relax.

When we got back, I sorted through my purchases, did yet more organising, prepped the dinner I'd missed out on the night before, then grabbed a beer and sat out on my camping chair. With my top off, Crocs kicked to the side, and Anxious curled up in the shade of the VW, I sighed as I sipped my beer, feeling more relaxed than I had since the trip began.

This truly was the life, and I had the whole long summer ahead of me.

The cold beer went down so well I decided to have another, so grabbed one from the tiny fridge, checked on dinner which was bubbling away nicely, and resumed my seat. Sipping the beer slowly, I thought about all I'd learned about this strange place and the occupants, as well as what I didn't know. It was definitely odd how some people acted, and I got the impression that there was more going on than I could possibly imagine. But places like this had a long history with small communities deeply entrenched in their ways, and as an outsider I couldn't possibly expect to understand or even be included in half of what was thought.

How honest was Bethan even being about the things she'd shared, or was she, too, keeping secrets? I wouldn't hold it against her if she was. We'd only just met after all. Plus, she was an officer of the law, even if a remarkably nice-smelling and rather talkative one.

I dozed in my chair for a while, smiling at the sounds of the children playing and the adults still bickering over tent poles or how burned the sausages were, then drifted off into a proper deep sleep. When I awoke half an hour later I felt refreshed, excited, and keen to continue doing nothing.

So there I remained, a man happy with his own company for the first time in years. Nobody to impress, nobody to worry about, nobody to get annoyed by or wish to be rather than myself. I was content being Max Effort, and it was a revelation. I could do this! I really could.

It felt like a spiritual experience. The understanding and acceptance was so deep I worried for a moment I was having a heart attack, but peace washed over me and I even accepted that.

If I was to die this very minute, then what better place to be?

All was well. All was right. All was as it should be.

And then I spied Barry Simms over by the shower blocks watching me. He turned away the moment he realised I'd seen him, pretending to read a poster tacked to the wall, but I knew he was spying on me and yet I couldn't bring myself to try to get answers from him. He was just an oddball. A strange man who maybe just wanted a friend, or maybe a shoulder to cry on. But I couldn't handle him and didn't want to break the spell, so I turned away and just waved as he walked across the field and glanced my way furtively. He waved back, then hurried to his camp then began fiddling with a disposable barbecue.

An hour later, dinner was ready, and Anxious and I were salivating at the prospect. With a fresh, crusty baguette bought from an artisan bakers—old habits died hard and no way could I bring myself to buy sliced white bread—and a pack of salted butter, I slid the soft golden goodness over the crumbly bread and let it melt for a few minutes in the sun while I dished up our dinner.

Tonight was a classic one-pot dish I'd always loved, especially because it gave me the chance to eat sausages. Not just any sausages mind you, these were from a local butchers, the sausages made on the premises from outdoor-reared rare-breed pigs, with sage and a hint of spice. I'd sampled them in the shop and they were right on the money for what I had in mind. With two duck legs also purchased, I had everything I needed. And now it was ready.

Cassoulet fit for two kings with empty bellies was served in our bowls and we tucked in eagerly. The duck was crispy on the outside, succulent inside, and the sausages were divine. The white beans went with it perfectly, the broth thick and unctuous. The crusty bread was the perfect accompaniment and I might have eaten rather more of it than I should have, but when it was so delicious how could I resist?

Anxious had a small second helping, I did the same, and the leftovers went into a container in the fridge for my lunch the following day. The bread would be hard by then, but I could toast it, so it was with a happy heart I did the dishes outside, then figured I should empty the grey waste water container from under the sink after I'd poured the dirty bowl of water into it. Feeling the weight of it, I changed my mind, and decided I would empty it on my way out the following morning, and top up with fresh water at the same time. That was the whole point about having a house on wheels—you didn't need to traipse back and forth across fields with everything. You could just jump out of the van to do it.

Feeling smug, I settled back down and let the atmosphere of the campsite envelop me. As the evening wore on, so it stilled, nothing but a gentle breeze and the sounds of the waves lapping against the shore far below.

Soon enough, darkness descended and the lights turned on at the shower and toilet blocks and the various stations for rubbish and water. People turned fairy lights or camping lights on at their plots and it was a magical time, like Christmas but without the need for a hat and gloves. I stayed up late into the night just enjoying the peace, hypnotised by the beauty.

When I finally stirred to go to bed, I groaned. I'd forgotten to sort the bed out again, and I hadn't got my torch out from the van either. I stumbled about, but found it easily enough, making a mental note to ensure I kept it somewhere handy from now on, and maybe set an alarm on my watch to remind me to sort out the bed earlier too. After a bit of a wrangle, I managed to get the contraption flat, and Anxious was straight up onto it and nabbed his spot with a groan as he closed his eyes.

Poor fella was exhausted. He loved the outdoors as much as me, but all this fresh air was taking some getting used to. Not that I would change it for anything. This was perfect, and I couldn't wait for the next day to begin.

I slept well, deep and sound, but at half four in the morning as the sunrise and the birds cried their welcome, I shot upright, realisation hitting me.

"I know who did it! How could I have been so dumb?"

Anxious barked at the noise, thinking there was something wrong, so I soothed him then opened up so we could both have a pee, oblivious to the fact I was stark naked until I was walking back to the van. Oh well, there was nobody else up anyway.

I glanced around just to check, but everyone else was sleeping, not a soul to be seen, so maybe now was the perfect time to fix this mess once and for all? Should I? Was it my place? Maybe I should wait until later?

After second-guessing myself for too long, I made the decision and felt better for it.

Even though it was an ungodly hour, I called Bethan and asked her to meet me in half an hour at the passing point further down the lane. She was understandably confused, but I asked her to trust me and I'd tell her everything once we met. She agreed, so I got myself ready then went to call on Mickey and Sue, the friendly couple who'd helped me out so much already.

After rapping on their campervan, I stood back and waited, feeling bad for rousing them so early, but knowing this had to be done now if the tentative plan still forming in my mind was going to work.

Mickey came out wearing nothing but his boxer shorts, scratching at his unmentionables, but he smiled when he saw me and stepped outside. Sue then came out right behind him and I apologised for the disturbance, but they were great about it and clearly knew something was up.

After explaining all I could, and asking them for a very large favour, they were instantly alert, eyes gleaming with excitement.

"You sure we're up to this? It's a bit epic, dude."

"I'm sure. Sorry to get you involved, but I know how much you love this place and how much you like Dai. And you get on well with Bethan, too, right?"

"Been watching that girl grow up for a few years. We come here at least twice a year and always have a chat with her, and we love Dai. Of course we'll help," said Sue.

"Sure we will. This is like a home to us. You can count on us."

"Thank you."

"Are you sure about this though?" asked Mickey with a frown. "It's pretty far-fetched, Max. Kinda epic, but utterly mad. You're certain?"

I took a moment to think about it, then admitted, "Not a hundred percent. Some of it, yes, I'm sure, but as for the rest, well, we'll just have to see what happens. But I've got this feeling and it's getting stronger, so I think so, yes, this is all true."

"Then let's go do this!" shouted Mickey.

"Ssh," hissed Sue. "You'll wake everyone."

We checked the site, but nobody emerged from their tents, although I did hear a grumble and see Barry Simms' tent shake a little.

After finalising a few more things, I left Mickey and Sue to it and returned to the campervan and Anxious who was waiting patiently beside his bowl, clearly expecting breakfast.

"We'll have to eat later, Anxious. We have important work to do and I want you on your best form. You're always faster and more alert on an empty tummy, so can you wait?"

With a mournful glance at his bowl, he looked into my eyes, full of trust and, yes, hope that I'd change my mind, then he grunted and began to wander off.

"How did you know we have to go up there first?" I asked as he headed for the path up to the cottage.

Anxious turned, cocked his head, then sighed.

Was it just me, or was he getting smarter by the day?

Chapter 16

I had half an hour before meeting Bethan, so knew I had to get my skates on. My insight upon waking this morning had come partly because of something I had hardly even registered at the time, but it had clearly been working away in my subconscious and now the idea refused to leave. Although the plan was already set in motion, I knew I had to check. Just so I'd be sure of myself when everything kicked off.

I huffed and puffed up the hill, with Anxious teasing me by running back and forth, seemingly able to do this all day if need be. I swiped my shoulder length hair behind my ears, still not quite used to it tickling my neck after so many years of it being short, and smiled to myself, knowing this was me now. Wilder, carefree, not conforming to convention and finally releasing the inner wild child I'd shut down for so many years in the pursuit of if not fame, then recognition and the perfection of my art.

Did I miss it? Yes, in many ways. I adored cooking, loved the way a dish came together. The planning, the execution, even giving orders in the kitchen. But I didn't miss the man it had made me. That had nothing to do with the work; it had everything to do with me. I became obsessive, single-minded, and utterly consumed. That's what it took to be the best, but at what cost to everything else in your life? The highest cost, as I'd discovered.

This was what I'd been missing my whole life. What I hadn't even realised I wanted or needed. To be let loose on the world, not confined in a back room with unbearable heat and too much stress. I would never give up cooking, never relinquish my love of good food and quality, properly sourced ingredients, but I could never be a chef again, never let myself get so involved in something that meant everything else suffered.

So here I was, panting my way up a hill to confirm a hunch I hoped would cement my conviction that I was about to reveal a killer.

What a turnaround? I chuckled to myself despite the seriousness of the situation, because I was loving this and felt so happy I could have shouted for joy if it wasn't such an ungodly hour. What was wrong with me? People were dead. Was it the adrenaline? The belief I was about to solve a real life, genuine crime? Was this how police officers felt? I believed they did, at least to some degree. Tinged with sadness and the acceptance that people weren't always good, was the underlying thrill of the chase, surely?

We made it to the top of the hill where the cottage was nestled in amongst the bracken and I hurried over to the cairn. I bent, and noted the smudges on the rocks, now more sure of myself than ever. Anxious came over and sniffed where I pointed, then began to lick the stone happily.

I couldn't resist a peek inside, even though I didn't expect to find anything. It was cleared out, nothing to see, but something made me crawl all the way in and sit there, the sudden cessation of sounds I hadn't even been aware of alarming.

Anxious sat between my legs for a moment, watching me, then shrugged and curled up with his head on my lap.

"You're so trusting. I enter a cave and you follow without question and now you're content just to lie there. Thank you for believing in me."

Anxious licked my knee.

I laughed, the echo in the cairn peculiar, but nice too. It was cool in here, but not damp, and strangely serene. I wondered why I wasn't freaked out by the fact a corpse had been hidden in here for many months, slowly degrading, eaten by the wild creatures of the hills.

Because that wasn't anything to be afraid of.

Dad had told me something many years ago that I guess I'd forgotten. He was forever giving me words of wisdom, some of which stuck, much of which hadn't. But this suddenly came to mind, and I said it out loud, just so I wouldn't forget the conversation again.

"Forget the saying that the dead can't hurt you, only the living can. It's not that at all."

"What is it then?"

"The living can be more cruel than you could possibly imagine. The dead just stink."

Dad had laughed, amused by his own words. I had just groaned, then wandered off to get a glass of milk.

"Come on, Anxious. Time to go inside the house. One more thing to check."

He was alert in an instant, then dashed off, yipping.

I crawled out behind him, squinting as the rising sun hit.

I headed towards the derelict cottage. It was truly beautiful in its own way, but with an air of sadness to it now I knew the full history. Was the woman who lived here her whole life happy? Was her existence so hard she never had the chance to even consider such things? Or was this her version of freedom? I suspected the latter, but would never know.

Anxious followed along happily, enjoying this game of ours, whatever it might be.

There wasn't much to investigate in here, as everything was covered in soot, or thick with the dust and grime of decades. I checked around anyway. The lime-washed stone was still relatively clean in places, and I traced a route around the room and stopped to inspect a few clear spots where the paint was still surprisingly pristine apart from the same smears as outside and on the tent and the box. It was a shame Anxious had licked them off, but I doubted it would have mattered anyway.

"We've got this, Anxious," I told my patient dog.

Seemingly pleased with this, he raced outside for a quick rabbit chase while I took the opportunity to sit on the wall and get my breathing under control.

He returned a few minutes later, devoid of rabbit, but panting happily and clearly thinking it was worth the chase anyway, so we made our way back down as the sun rose and the day began to warm. My feet were soaked from the dew but I didn't care, and if anything it made me feel more connected than ever to this wonderful place and the amazing people I'd met.

I'd always been a bit of a loner, and not great in the company of others, an introvert who needed time alone to feel connected to the world, but also someone who was quite jovial and outgoing once I was in the mood. The way I was now came as quite a surprise, and I realised that was because I wasn't over-thinking things or second-guessing my own and everyone else's next move or comment and it was another revelation. Doing this was good for me. I wasn't big on soul-searching, but it was opening up new insights into my own life and personality that I guess maybe I hadn't had time to reflect on until Min and I separated, but even then I refused to look too deeply into myself for fear of what I might find.

What surprised me the most was that I was enjoying the man I was, who I had become, and that had to be worth more than anything else, right?

Soon enough, I found we were almost back at the campsite, so Anxious raced down the last section of path and burst into the field, then tore across the grass and disappeared around the van.

I caught him up only to find him sitting, waiting, eyes on me.

"Sorry little buddy, but you still need to wait. Remember what I said about you working best on an empty stomach so you have the speed? Well, that still stands. Time to go."

Anxious looked from me to his bowl, then back again, before sighing then jumping into the van. He sat on the passenger seat and cocked his head, clearly wondering why I was still hanging around.

"Thank you," I laughed, as amazed as always by how smart he was.

Soon enough, we were off to catch a killer.

After sorting out the gate as quietly as I could, already wincing after driving the rather loud VW across the top of the field at such an hour, I parked up where I'd arranged to meet Bethan and waited, my nerves increasing the longer I sat there. She pulled up soon enough and I got out to greet her; she did not look happy. Or very awake.

"Sorry about the time," I said lamely.

"That's fine. It doesn't matter. But go over this one more time so I can get it straight in my head. And are you sure about this?"

"Yes, I'm sure." I explained what I'd just done, and my reasoning behind what I'd told her on the phone, then I revealed the final missing piece of the puzzle before asking, "Are you alright? I know it's a lot to take in."

"I'm fine. Max, I've had my suspicions but didn't really want to believe any of this. I've been trying to figure this all out, but it's been hard without all the information the detectives have, and it's so close to home. This is family, you understand? Family."

"I know, and I'm sorry. Maybe I'm wrong. Maybe this is all one big mistake?"

"You don't really believe that, do you?"

"No, I don't."

Bethan sighed, then she tucked a curl behind her ear, smiled sadly, checked her uniform and gear, then said, "So let's do this. We'll take the van, just in case anyone spots us, but we'll park well before anyone could hear, and don't turn on your lights."

"Yes, ma'am," I said, saluting now she was all business.

Bethan shook her head, smiling despite herself, and just said, "Come on. And Max?"

"Yes?"

"Thank you."

"Hang in there, kiddo. This will be over with soon enough."

I managed to get us up the steep climb without incident, Vee straining in low gear but making a valiant effort before I pulled onto the flat and she farted in relief. At least, that's what it sounded like. I never imagined I'd have a flatulent campervan, but this old machine was full of surprises.

With the engine off and the handbrake on, we got out and closed the doors quietly then took a circuitous route up the rest of the hill until we could see the polytunnels shining in the morning sun. Bethan pointed to the dirty Transit so we headed over to it, hunched and fast to minimise being seen, and I don't think I breathed until we were safely out of sight.

This was so close to ending now that my adrenaline was surging, a buzzing in my system that made me feel weirdly elated and almost desperate to shout out something stupid and spoil it all. Bethan was rosy-cheeked and clearly feeling it too. She smiled, her eyes twinkling, but there was a deep sadness, too, because the poor woman knew her life would never be the same again.

There was no going back, no way to make this a happy ending for everyone, but there had to be justice and there had to be a reckoning.

We nodded to each other, and just as we moved a noise caused us to stop and hide again.

Footsteps approached, and my heart hammered in my chest. We needed everyone together, and we needed events to unfold as planned. Bethan put her hand to my arm and shook her head. I nodded in agreement; now was not the time to do anything. We held our breath as the van door opened and someone rummaged inside then closed it with a loud thud that set my heart to racing even faster.

Then the footsteps retreated and I risked a quick peek. It was Hywel with a crate full of trays for the strawberries. I had to hand it to them. They sure worked hard and with incredibly long hours.

Ducking back to Bethan, I whispered, "We should wait a few minutes. Your dad might come back. Hywel's just collecting trays. How many do they pick a day?"

"Hundreds of them. It's really tough work and even with the rows of plants at waist height it still plays havoc with your back. I think that's why Grandad is so hunched over. He spent decades picking crops from the fields as some things just aren't suited to machines. It's why he gave up on it all, but my parents thought this would be a winner."

"Sounds rough."

"It is. Listen, is someone coming?"

We stood stock still and strained our ears as possibly Hywel returned and again rocked the van. Anxious looked from me to the van but remained seated, and I bent to stroke his head to ensure he didn't do anything to blow our cover. I knew he would behave, he always did, but the stakes were high and I cursed not bringing his lead just to be on the safe side.

Once Hywel was gone and we'd waited several more minutes, I knew Bethan felt the time was right. She was beginning to sweat, and was getting itchy feet as she kept shuffling around.

"Are you ready?"

"As ready as I'll ever be."

With no more reasons to wait, we strode from our hiding place, shoulders squared, and marched towards the polytunnel I saw Hywel enter. Suddenly, I stopped, thinking I heard a noise, checking behind me for fear of being walloped over the head.

"What's up?" whispered Bethan, eyes darting.

"Nothing. Just getting jittery. Don't rush this, and don't go shouting."

"Why would I shout?"

"Because this is nuts and I'm seriously wondering what I've got you involved in."

"Unless you're forgetting something, I'm the law around here. You aren't getting me into anything. I'm deciding to pursue this and letting you come along."

"That's the spirit," I said, smiling, then I steeled myself for the showdown.

Chapter 17

The lights blazed at the polytunnels, although I very much doubted that anyone apart from Bernard, Gwen, and Hywel were there so early. But there was a chance people might have been hauled in to keep the work going. We'd just have to risk it.

"Let's be quiet, okay?" I whispered as we crept forward.

"They'll know we're here soon enough, so what difference does it make?"

"We don't want them to bolt, remember? Last thing we need is chasing around the fields before it's even properly light yet. And look how much power they must be using. It must be costing Dai a fortune."

"He's always grumbling about how the electricity bill is making it impossible for him to make a living. I just assumed it had gone up the same as everyone else's. It's more than double what it used to be."

"Yes, and I bet he had a few lulls a while back before it suddenly went through the roof again, right?"

"Maybe. I don't really remember. Grandad is always complaining about something or other so I don't aways pay attention like I should. It's what farmers do best."

"That's understandable. He is rather an oddball."

Bethan frowned and cocked her head. "An oddball? Really? He's a total sweetie. I never saw him like that."

"You didn't? Must just be me then. It's probably as you said. He likes to put on a show for the guests. Make it a memorable visit by always acting different every time you see him. He's mellowed slightly since I arrived, but I'm still never sure what he's going to do. One minute he's sweet as pie, the next he's snapping at me and being super grumpy."

Bethan laughed. "Yes, that's Grandad alright. He's such a character. Max, are you sure about this? I don't even really understand what you've been telling me. Taking power from Grandad? That's awful, and I'll put a stop to it, but are you sure about the rest?"

"Positive. Just hang in there if it gets gnarly, and I promise you'll get your arrest. You're going to be big news around here once this gets out, but are you ready for the aftermath?"

"How do you mean?"

"I mean, your family is involved in this. I'm sorry to say, but things will never be the same again for any of you. It might be a bit much."

"I can handle it."

"If you're sure?"

Bethan nodded, face determined. "I am. Max, two people are dead, and that's not right. We need to put a stop to this before anyone else is killed. I still can't believe this, but we need to do what's right."

"We do. But I know if it was my family I'd be a mess of indecision right about now."

"Not me. I'm ready."

"Then let's do this. Everything should be set up by now, so remember, play it cool, don't push it too fast, and get ready to use your superhero belt." I nodded to the utility belt strapped around her waist, marvelling at the shiny black objects and the leather pouches.

"It's not a superhero belt, silly," she chuckled. "Every officer wears one, and it's not like they've given us guns."

"No, and that's probably for the best. If the police have guns, then that means the bad guys will too."

With a nod to each other, we skirted around the van and I couldn't help note the damp morning air up here where it was higher and more exposed to the elements. Dew clung to the grass on the Welsh mountainside, an intricate shimmer of gossamer spiders' webs carpeting the whole field like a faint silver blanket. But already the sun was warming the air, and as the breeze brushed past us lazily I knew that in an hour or so the ground would be dry and hard once again.

Anxious did as I asked and remained by my side, then I gave the command and he shot off.

It was just me and Bethan now. Time to put an end to this madness.

"...don't care," came the muffled voice of Hywel. "If I can get the work then I should do it."

"And what about here?" shrieked Gwen. "You expect me and Bernard to do everything? We're overwhelmed as it is."

"It wasn't my idea to set all this up. It was you two. This was your idea. I told you it was too much, that there's no money in it, but oh no, you both insisted you could make it work, that it would be cheap to run and would make a real difference."

"And it is. I told you, it's making a profit."

"So you say. But you won't let me see the books, will you? It's so damn secretive. I just want to see what the actual profit is. I'm not dumb. I can figure out the numbers easily enough."

"It's the most profitable thing we have going on right now," said Bernard, a voice of calm and reason whilst the other two were clearly beyond frustrated with not only the business, but each other by the sounds of it.

I pulled Bethan aside and asked, "Are they always like this?"

"Usually, yes. It's got worse over the years, but it's pretty standard. I can't tell you how many times I've expected them to leave each other. One of them is always storming off. Dad has it the worst. Mum's always on at him. Max, can we please just get this over and done with? And are you certain about all of this?"

"I think so. But look, I'm no policeman. This is all just a hunch."

"You haven't even explained everything. Think maybe now is the time?" she asked, glancing back at the polytunnel and the raised voices.

"A few minutes and it will all be over. You're doing amazing, kiddo," I said, smiling in sympathy for what was obviously a very difficult time for her.

With a deep breath, Bethan squared her shoulders, smiled sadly, and said, "Okay. I'm trusting you, Max, so please don't let me down."

With a nervous gulp, I said, "I'll try not to. Be brave, and you're doing great."

Checking that Anxious was still waiting outside the polytunnel, we approached.

From the doorway, the lights strung along the endless rows of strawberries on raised platforms so they could be picked without

138

getting on your knees made me think of Christmas. The sweet smell of ripe strawberries was almost overpowering, sickly as it caught in the back of my throat.

Gwen, Hywel, and Bernard were partway down an aisle, still bickering. Anxious barked after a signal from me, and they turned their attention our way.

"Bethan, what are you doing here?" asked Hywel. "And so early too?"

"And why is that man with you?" asked Gwen with a scowl as she crossed her arms.

"He's here because he knows what you did. What you all did?" Bethan gulped, but then she puffed out her chest, and added, "Mum, you've got some explaining to do. And so does he!" She pointed at Bernard, who looked to Gwen for help, but she had eyes only for her daughter.

"What's this nonsense? Be about your business, girl. We have things to do. Work to be done. And your father," she almost spat the words, "can't be bothered to help."

"I told you already, I have work with e-energy today. I can't blow them off. I'm trying to get a full-time position with them and it's been months since they gave me a day's work. If I don't show, they'll never give me another chance."

"It's okay, Dad, you should go. You need the money and I don't want you to miss out on it."

"He's going to have to hear this, Bethan," I said softly, feeling bad for Hywel, but maybe they'd understand.

"What's going on, love?" asked Hywel. "Why are you looking so angry? And what is this about? It's six in the morning. You shouldn't be here. And no offence, Max, but what have you got my daughter involved in?"

"It's not me whose got her involved in anything," I said. "It's Gwen and Bernard you can thank for that."

Hywel frowned as he turned to Gwen. "What's he talking about?" Then he spun to Bernard and asked, "Bernard? Do you know what this is about?"

"No idea," he mumbled, eyes darting past us. His fists bunched and colour rose up his neck, but he didn't move.

"Max figured it out," said Bethan so softly it was hard to hear her.

"What was that?" called Hywel.

"Come closer, all of you," snapped Bethan. "And I said Max figured it out."

"Not all of it. Just some."

Hywel, who was a little behind the others, pushed them forward until they moved of their own volition, then they paused halfway to us.

"Let's start with the electrics," I said. "Hywel, I take it you didn't know that the power for everything up here is being stolen from Dai?"

"How'd you mean? This is a new business venture and had its own install. Otherwise, it would be linked in with the campsite. We run the farm separate. This is our business, that's his."

"No, it's not, Dad. The only reason this is making any money at all is because Mum's been stealing from Grandad."

"That can't be right. I'd know. I'm an electrician."

"But you aren't here that often," said Bethan. "When it was set up, Mum and Bernard got some e-electric guy to bodge the install and change the wiring. But there was an accident and someone got hurt so he swapped it back. He didn't want to risk his job. But I'm guessing Bernard redid it and now they're stealing the power from Grandad again. He keeps complaining about how ridiculous his electricity bill is, but I never really took much notice what with the price hikes."

"You're talking nonsense, girl," snapped Gwen. "Who put such fancy ideas into your head? I bet it was you, wasn't it?" she hissed, glaring at me.

"It's easy enough to check, and if we're right, you'll be in a world of trouble. It's theft, and there are heavy fines for tampering with meters and causing a risk to life. Not only do you all work here, but you have staff too."

"Bernard, is this true?" asked Hywel.

"I'm saying nothing," he grunted.

"It's no use denying it," said Bethan. "Dad, I'm sorry, but at first I thought it must have been you as you're the one with ties to e-electric. But it wasn't, it was Bernard. I'm sorry."

"I don't understand. I don't know what you're talking about," said Hywel, rubbing at his cheek. "Why would your mum steal from her own father? Why would she risk anyone getting hurt?" Once again, he confronted his wife. "Gwen?"

"Fine," she sighed. "We got a guy to hook us up to Dad's meter. Then Bernard made a few changes up here once it was done. But there was a slight accident, nothing too bad, but the installer heard about it. He came and changed everything back, as he was panicked. Stupid man ranted about the work Bernard had done up here, as if he didn't know what he was doing. We were losing so much money, though, that Bernard switched back to Dad's meter so we could keep making a profit. Do you know how much power it takes to keep these tunnels warm with the weather all over the place?"

"No, because you never let me see the books. And now I know why!" Hywel raged, slamming a fist down on the strawberries, flatting them. He lifted his hand and looked at it then let it drop to his side. "Sorry, I shouldn't have got angry."

"It's okay, Dad, I understand. Mum, why would you do that? You know Grandad's struggling."

"He's struggling! Ha, that's rich. We're on the poverty line working all these hours and he's finding it a little difficult, is he? He could sell and we'd be millionaires."

"Which brings us on to the next thing," I said, knowing this was going to be so hard.

"Dad, can I ask you something?" said Bethan nervously, wringing her hands.

"Of course, love," he said, shaking his head at the confusion he felt.

"When you worked for e-energy, did they give you a van?"

"It was a beauty! They like to make a good impression and it's free advertising. I nearly always got a van."

"One with all the tools and meters, and uniforms inside?" I asked.

"Yes. How else would I be able to do the work?"

"So it wouldn't really be noticed if, say, someone took a uniform or two out of the van?" I asked.

"I guess not. There are usually a few in them. They've vans especially for the temps and they're kitted out a bit differently. Less expensive tools, but always with a few sizes of boiler suits and what have you."

"So Mum or Bernard could have taken a few of them and you wouldn't notice?"

"Not really. I never even thought about it. What are you getting at? I don't understand."

"Remember that we found e-electric clothes up at the old cottage," Bethan reminded him.

"Sure."

"Mum and Bernard put them there."

"I don't need to stand here and listen to this." Bernard grabbed his jacket from a peg on the side of the row and began to surge forward.

Hywel grabbed him by his upper arm, fingers like a vice, and yanked him to a stop. "You aren't going anywhere until Bethan's finished talking. Understand?" he growled.

"You can't expect me to stay and let her rant like that." Bernard tugged at Hywel's grip but it was clear he was outmatched by the stronger man.

"You will. Carry on, Bethan."

"They put the boiler suits there. The rest is more conjecture, but Max and I are guessing that either Mum or Bernard had made a fire in the hearth, most likely to burn clothes, and the other came and put it out then stuffed the IDs and the boiler suit up the chimney."

"Most likely it was you, Bernard," I said. "That's why the IDs were so high up. I couldn't understand why, but you're a tall man, so I'm pretty sure you did it. Quite a good hiding place, but why the boiler suit?"

"To stop the smoke, right?" asked Bethan.

"This is nonsense," shouted Bernard. "Why on earth would we do such a thing? Why would we even have the boiler suits and the IDs? You aren't making sense, either of you."

"He's right," said Gwen, a wicked smile on her face. "You're just making this up. What possible reason would either of us have for doing such a thing? Bethan, my love, I know you want to get ahead as a police officer, but accusing your own parents of, well, I'm not quite sure what you're accusing us of, isn't the way to get ahead."

"I'm accusing you of murder, Mum. Murder!" screamed Bethan as tears rolled down her blotchy cheeks.

"Murder?" asked Hywel. "You can't be serious?"

"Deadly," I said. "Hywel, I don't think you had anything to do with this, but if you did, now is the time to own up."

"None of this is making any sense to me," he said. "But I didn't have any part in it."

"Dad didn't know," said Bethan. "He's honest, and would never even think of cheating Grandad, let alone stealing."

"So, it was Bernard who put the stolen uniforms and the IDs up the chimney," I said. "It was going around and around in my head as to why anyone would want the uniforms if they didn't intend to use them to enter people's homes and steal from them. But then it hit me. What if they didn't want to use them to steal from anyone. Not things, anyway. What if they needed them as a way to gain access to someone's property and mess with the wiring?"

"Now you aren't making sense," said Bernard, a sly smile creeping across his tanned face. "One minute you accuse me of doing the wiring, now you're saying I went in disguise. Dai knows me. He'd recognise me."

"Of course he would," I agreed. "But not if you got someone to dress in the uniform and followed the instructions you gave them. My best guess is you got one of the poor men you give work to here to do the change for you. Dai would let him in if he said it was to check on the new meter as he kept reporting the prices to the electricity company. He'd leave the guy to his work and wouldn't know it was an impostor."

"Now you're just babbling," said Gwen. "I don't want to hear another word about this nonsense. I'm leaving."

She stormed forward, but Bethan stepped in front of her and said, "I know it was you, Mum, and I have proof."

Gwen paused, her eye twitching, then she grinned and said, "You have no proof, love. I know that for a fact."

"Is that right?" I asked.

"How?"

"Because I didn't do it of course! Now let me out!"

Bethan grabbed her mother's arm and spun her around, then pushed her back towards the others. "Nobody goes anywhere until this is done. You got someone to fiddle with the wiring after the genuine installer put things back how they should be. And then there was another accident, right? One of the homeless men, I suppose. He died, so you stuffed the body in the cairn and left him there. You left a man up there."

"It... it's not what you think," stammered Bernard, looking away from Gwen when she snarled at him. "It was an accident. He just keeled over one day and died. We didn't hurt him. But we couldn't report it as the workers are strictly off the books. It's cash in hand, no questions asked. If we reported it we'd be shut down and the whole enterprise would be ruined."

"Stop talking," hissed Gwen.

"No, this has gone on long enough. I want to come clean, tell the whole story."

"Then why don't you start at the beginning," I demanded.

Chapter 18

"None of this was my idea," sighed Bernard.

"Shut up, you fool!" hissed Gwen, gouging at his face.

Luckily, Hywel grabbed her arm before she took an eye out and gripped her tight. "Do not move and do not speak. Let him say what he has to. Our Bethan knows what you both did, so there's no point pretending, but I want to hear."

"I will not stay here and be accused of... of what, murder?" raged Gwen.

"Mum, if you don't be quiet, and if you try to run away, then I will never, ever forgive you, understand?"

"But I'm innocent," she pleaded.

"Then shut up! I will handcuff you if you try to hurt anyone or run."

"You're no child of mine," Gwen muttered, but she lowered her arms and Hywel released her.

"It wasn't my idea," Bernard repeated, getting a scowl from Gwen.

"We decided to set up the soft fruit, but then we got bad weather and it all began to go wrong. We needed the income, so we got this idea to borrow Dai's electric. I knew a guy, and he swapped over the install when the new meter was put in, but as you say, someone got hurt because I'd already messed with things up here. Everything got switched back, and we couldn't have that. Gwen took the uniforms from Hywel's van, and I copied his ID then made some fake ones. We never knew who we would get working for us, so I made a few, and yes, I got one of the workers to do as I instructed and change the power supply back over."

"And the man in the cairn? You said he died here?" I asked.

144

"It was an accident, I swear. He just keeled over and was gone. We panicked, so hid the body up there. We were nervous wrecks for days, then weeks, then we just kind of forgot about it and moved on with our lives. I assumed it was sealed up and nobody would ever find him. I guess I was wrong." Bernard hunched his shoulders, trying to make himself small, as though he could hide from the things he'd done.

"And you put everything up the chimney?" I asked.

"Yes, because somebody," he darted a glance at Gwen, "was trying to burn clothes and draw attention. I took them from the fire, bagged them up, and then stuffed the uniforms up the chimney."

"But why did you have more uniforms and still have the IDs?"

"I kept hold of them just in case," admitted Bernard. "When I bumped into Ian, the man from e-energy and he said he'd heard what I'd done about the power and was going to turn it back how it should be, I figured we'd need them so brought them here."

"But who's the dead man that Max found?" asked Hywel. "How does that tie in?"

"That was nothing to do with me," said Bernard. "That was her idea."

"You're the one who killed him!" spat Gwen, whirling.

"And you're the one who decided to use it to disgrace your own father. It's disgusting. You think I was going to stay with you once you got all the money? Well, you were wrong. I'd leave you in a heartbeat once I got the cash."

I'd known it was coming, but it was still a shock, especially to Hywel and Bethan.

"You two were cheating on me?" Hywel almost whispered. "You were having an affair?"

"Of course we were, you idiot!" snapped Gwen. "If you weren't so stupid you'd have known about it years ago. I only keep you around so we can get more work done. But I thought me and Bernard had a deal. We'd get Dad to sell up then we'd be able to retire, and you'd be out of the picture."

"Mum, how could you?" sobbed Bethan. She wiped away the tears, turned to Bernard, and said, "What happened?"

"It was early morning, and I was coming to begin work up here. I didn't even see him. I just... I just... He was standing in the middle of the road. I slammed on the brakes, and you should have seen his face. He thought he was going to die. I jumped out, thinking I'd hit him, but he was fine, not a scratch on him. A walker partway through a hiking holiday was what I guessed. He had enough stuff with him for weeks, and he had maps of the whole coastline. He'd come from John o' Groats and was going to do the walk to Land's End. At least, I assumed so."

"But he was okay?" asked Bethan.

"Yes, for a moment, then his eyes rolled up and he collapsed. I couldn't find a pulse and he was dead. I called Gwen and she came right over and then she had her idea. We wrapped him in his tent, stuck him on the roof and were going to drive to the campsite and dump him just outside the gates. But he must have slid off the roof. We left him there and got away before anyone saw."

"He wasn't dead," I said. "Tell them, Bethan."

"That man was still alive. He almost suffocated in the tent, but it was the fall that killed him. He broke his neck. You both killed him. You killed an innocent man and you covered up the death of another. All so you could make money and all so you could try to force Grandad to give up his home."

"It was all an accident!" pleaded Bernard. "The man we hid at the cairn just died. We didn't want any questions. And yes, we were using the other body to scare people away, hope it got into the papers and Dai would sell up, but I didn't know he was still alive."

"You cheated on me," mumbled Hywel, dazed. "You broke our home apart. You cheated your own father, you betrayed your family, and you treated human beings like little more than things. How could you?"

"Oh shut up, Hywel!" screamed Gwen. "And you... you... Ugh, I can't even be bothered to talk to you. I deny all knowledge of this. None of this is true, and I had nothing to do with any of it. You can't prove it, and no daughter of mine will testify against me, right, love?" asked Gwen, softening her voice and smiling.

"Mum, you were never nice to me and Dad as I was growing up. Dad always looked after me while you schemed and plotted and tried to earn money with your dumb ideas rather than hard work, and now you've gone too far. You betrayed us all. And I will testify."

"So will I if need be," I said.

"No, you've done enough, Max. We have all we need."

"What are you talking about?" asked Gwen. "I will never say I was involved. I will deny it. You can say whatever you want. It's your word against mine."

"You're forgetting something, dear wife," said Hywel.

"What?" she hissed.

"I most definitely will testify against you. And if I'm not mistaken, so will Bernard."

"I'm not going down for this on my own, no way. Gwen, most of this was your idea, so you're even more to blame than me. I'm going to tell the whole truth. I never meant to kill anyone, but if we did, then we have to accept the consequences." Bernard faced Hywel and said, "Sorry to go behind your back like this. I liked Gwen at first, then realised just how nasty a piece of work she was. I just wanted the money."

Hywel nodded, then he punched Bernard in the face and he dropped like a rock.

"Will I get into trouble for doing that?" he asked, rubbing his hand.

"No, you won't, Dad, because who would tell?"

"Not me," I said, shaking my head.

Anxious, who had remained silent throughout, howled as he ran over to Hywel and pawed at his leg. Hywel bent and scratched behind his ear, Anxious' tail spinning madly.

"He knows an honest man when he meets one," I said.

"You'll still never make this stick," insisted Gwen. "Everyone will just think my daughter has it in for me."

"Mum, that's where you're wrong." Bethan and I looked past them to the back of the polytunnel where Mickey and Sue gave us the thumbs up, grinning from ear to ear, then stood aside and revealed a veritable army of police, detectives, and if I wasn't mistaken, was that Barry Simms too? I rubbed my tired eyes, but then there was no sign of him. I must have him on the brain.

Everyone turned at the commotion as the police moved forward. Bernard remained where he was, but Gwen made a run for it.

Anxious, always keen to bite an ankle if it's allowed, spun at my whistle and I said, "Sick 'em," and pointed at Gwen. He was off like a shot, and before she could even reach us, Anxious had his teeth clamped down on her ankle and she fell face first into the hard ground. Anxious shook his head from side to side as Gwen screamed, so I called him off and he sauntered over, a cocky swagger, brimming with pride.

"Well done," I told him, and gave him a biscuit. Satisfied his work was done, he went outside to eat in peace. I turned to Bethan and said, "And well done to you too. You did amazingly well, especially as it's your mum. I'm so sorry, but at least we know."

"Yes, at least we know," she sighed, smiling weakly.

An officer read Gwen and Bernard their rights, then they were marched past us in handcuffs. Neither even looked at us.

Once the arrests were made, and things settled down, only the three of us remained inside the polytunnel.

"I'll leave you both alone," I said. "Sorry this got so messy, Hywel."

"Yeah, me too. But thank you. You did what you had to, but it wasn't malicious, it just needed to be done."

"Sorry, Dad."

"Don't be. You're the only one I truly care about, and that's always been true. You'll always be my little girl, and nothing will change that. Ever."

I left them to it as they embraced.

Gwen was giving the officers serious grief, ranting and raving and generally refusing to accept that she'd been caught. Not only had she been heard by us, but by Mickey and Sue and a whole horde of other officers. There was no denying her involvement, and absolutely no chance of her denial being believed.

Bernard was rather more stoic. He clearly admitted his role in this whole sorry mess and would no doubt accept his punishment.

"That was awesome, dude," gushed Mickey as he and Sue came over.

"I don't know about that," I said wearily.

"No, it was incredible," agreed Sue. "You were great. And did you really figure everything out on your own?"

"Not all of it, but things began to click into place once I spoke to a man about doing dodgy wiring up here. That was the start of it, anyway. Then I just got to thinking, and it really bugged me about the IDs being up high in the chimney."

Mickey and Sue exchanged a confused glance, then Mickey laughed and said, "Mate, we have no idea what you're talking about. All we know is that you wanted us to go get the police and come up to the polytunnels on foot and listen at the back. We don't know what you've been up to. But a lot by the sounds of it."

"Yes, quite a lot. Thanks once again. Come over later and I'll make dinner, if you fancy? I'm doing one-pot meals every night, and I'll do something special."

"Sounds awesome," gushed Mickey.

"We'll be there," agreed Sue.

I watched them leave, along with the police vans, cars, and Bernard and Gwen along with them. Soon it was just me, Anxious, Hywel, and Bethan.

"What now?" I asked.

"I'll go down to the station and help sort out this mess. I can't believe this is happening. How could Mum do this to her own family?"

"Desperation? She wanted a different life and couldn't find a way to get it."

"So she turned on her own?"

"I guess."

"Poor Grandad. He'll be distraught about this."

"He's a tough old guy. He can handle it. He's got you, and I think that's what keeps him going."

"You might be right."

"So, you got your first arrest?"

"No, I didn't. No way could I arrest Mum, so other officers did it. I'm still a zero."

"Maybe not for long. I bet you'll be moving up soon enough after this."

"Max, you deserve the credit and I'll make sure you get it."

"Oh no, you keep me out of this as much as possible. I'll come and give a statement, but that's all. As far as I'm concerned, this was your idea. You followed the clues, put the pieces together, and here we are."

"Well, thank you, that's very kind. Shall we go?"

"Yes, that sounds great."

Hywel was silent, most likely numb with shock, trailing behind Bethan like a puppy after its mother.

At the campsite, Bethan went to break the news to Dai, while Hywel remained outside, so I left them to it. I invited her for dinner that evening and she promised she'd come if she could.

All the excitement had made me famished, so Anxious and I finally got our breakfast after I had a coffee, then I headed up to check on Dai. It must have been a huge shock for him, so I wanted to make sure the old fella was coping.

I found him outside, just pottering about not doing much of anything. He looked a little lost.

"Dai, how are you?"

"Eh? Oh, it's you," he scowled, then hobbled over, still an impressive man despite the hunch.

"Yes, it's me. I assume Bethan told you what happened?"

"Yes, she did. Terrible business. They got what they deserved, so that's for the best."

"You aren't upset? I mean, what Gwen did? It must be quite a shock."

Dai lifted his head and held my gaze; a single tear fell and he made no move to wipe it away.

Then I understood.

"You knew, didn't you?"

"Only some of it. Not about the poor men. But I knew about the electricity. I'm not an idiot. When the guy from town came to put the smart meter in, I didn't think anything of it, but when the bills started coming in, I took a look and knew it was wrong. Then he came back and I got suspicious. When another man came and seemed utterly incompetent, I was sure it was Gwen who was trying to steal from me. I let it be. She's blood, and was desperate."

"So you left them to take your power?"

"Yes. It was that or have it out with her. She's hard-headed enough as it is. Just like her dad," he huffed, "and I couldn't handle the upset. I want a quiet life, Max. At my age you just want peace. I know I haven't got long and I want to enjoy it. But it seems she wasn't happy with just stealing from me. She wanted to drive me out of business too. Leaving bodies in the road to cause a stir. What was she thinking?"

"It's social media and review sites, Dai. As soon as the word got out, it would be all over the review sites that people were dying here. It would put visitors off and make you more inclined to sell if business went bad."

"So those reviews will already be up, I guess?"

"I honestly haven't looked, but my guess is Gwen and Bernard would have been the ones writing them. It would snowball. It's easy enough to make a load of email addresses and post all over the internet. It might have worked. But it won't now the whole mess has been sorted out."

"Thanks to you."

"No, thanks to Bethan. She put a lot of it together and came up with a way to get them to talk. You should be proud."

"I am. So proud. I wish Gwen could have been a better mother, a better daughter, and a better wife. I blame myself."

"You shouldn't. Some people are just like that. It's no reflection on you."

"Son, I know you mean well, but you try saying that to any parent whose child has gone off the rails and you'll get the same answer. They wished they could have done things differently. They did something wrong. They should have tried harder. How can you not blame yourself when it's your own flesh and blood?"

"I guess you're right. I didn't mean any offence."

"And none taken. Thank you for everything you've done. I appreciate it. Now bugger off, will you? I need to get the mower out and tidy up the field. We've got a busy day today, and I want it to look its best."

"You bet. And Dai?"

"What now?" he grumbled.

"Bethan will make a great campsite owner. She's smart, easy to get on with, bright and positive, and she smells bloody lovely."

"She does smell nice, doesn't she?" Dai winked, then turned his back and wandered over to the cottage. The door closed quietly and I heard him sob.

Anxious whined, but there was nothing we could do. Some things needed to be worked out as a family, and Bethan would always be there for him.

Chapter 19

Anxious and I were antsy after the peculiar and very intense morning, so we headed off to the beach to clear our heads and try to enjoy ourselves. It was hard, as I felt so bad for poor Bethan and her father and grandad. But, and I hated to admit it, I was proud of myself.

After years of thinking of nothing but menus and the bottom line, it felt good to do something for others. I wasn't half bad at it either. I'd managed to put the pieces together, and that was no mean feat. Maybe luck had a part to play, but as they say, you make your own luck in this world. I'd asked questions, followed leads, and worked out at least some of it before we confronted Gwen.

I hadn't known how the two men had died, but suspected it had to be Gwen and Bernard once I saw how they looked at each other and seeing that Hywel was a genuine guy. But maybe that was just me wanting to think I was a proper detective, when the real giveaway was the stain on the tent I hadn't even thought about until this morning when it suddenly clicked into place. It was then I suspected him and Gwen.

Who would have thought that a simple juice stain would lead to me uncovering a plot to discredit a campsite owner in order to get his money?

It was done, and what came next was out of my hands.

The sun shone, people were already arriving for a day on the beach, and a few brave groups of women were even swimming. I wondered what that would be like. You heard about it all the time now, people extolling the virtues of cold water swimming like it was a new religion. I guessed everyone needed faith in one form or another. Something to give them hope, to give them joy, to make life worthwhile. And it was. What a beautiful world we got the opportunity to play in!

We chatted with other dog owners, we sniffed a few bums, and we chased after balls. Some of that is even true. Anxious and I were carefree, like little children as we raced around in circles and splashed in the shallows, enjoying ourselves like this was the last day on earth. And what if it was? What if this was to be my last day?

Then I'd done a good job and looked after those who I cared about most.

Which reminded me.

I pulled out my phone and called home. Mum and Dad wanted to know every last detail, so I filled them in on it all and they gasped, interrupted, and congratulated, which I knew they would. Once Mum had gone to check on their breakfast, I spoke to Dad for a few minutes in private and he asked about Min and how it had gone. I told him the truth, and he sympathised, but then he said the strangest thing, and it will stay with me for all of my days.

"You get what you want in this life by never giving up. You don't get what you deserve, you get what you fight for. What are you going to fight for, Son?"

We spoke for a while longer, then I said my thanks for the words of wisdom and hung up.

"What are we going to fight for, Anxious?" I asked him.

Anxious looked to me, then the ball at my feet, and barked.

"I guess you already know how to get what you want. Maybe I should start doing the same?"

After throwing the ball, I sent a nervous text message to Min.

I'll never give up chasing the ball. I will fight until it's thrown.

I pressed send before I changed my mind, then wondered what the hell I was doing. How cryptic was that? She wouldn't have a clue what I was talking about. She'd think I'd lost the plot or was trying to wind her up. What a muppet!

Several seconds later, my phone beeped. I cringed as I opened up the message, expecting the worst.

Maybe I'll throw it one day. Just not today. The ball is scared and confused.

Rather than push my luck, I just sent an X.

Damn, was that right? Maybe I should have sent a proper reply?

Leave it alone, Max, don't over think this.

After a nice long stroll to the far end of the beach, we played in the rock pools. I turned over rocks and Anxious dove in after the crabs and tiny fish, barking his attack so they'd wilt under his might. It didn't work out, but he had fun trying and it lifted my spirits no end. Once the local population of crustaceans were firmly put in their place, we made a few stops in town to gather supplies, then headed back to the campsite.

Business certainly hadn't been affected and the place was very busy, but everyone had room and everyone was happy, so I spent the afternoon preparing everything for dinner, unsure who would come, then letting it simmer for as long as possible. Not knowing what anyone liked, I went for a simple one-pot dish of a thick beef stew with onions and carrots, plus more bread from the bakery as it was just too delicious.

I dozed, I giggled into my hand at the newbies trying to pitch tents, and marvelled at the new blow-up tents that seemed very cool if rather bulky to handle. Families even had tiny tall tents now for a portable toilet, and I considered getting one but was soon put off when I saw one blow over when an unexpected gust swept through, causing carnage and a very rapid change of clothes for an unfortunate woman.

Dai drove around and around, mowing the grass, checking for litter, and chatting to people, happy doing what he loved, but with an unmistakable air of sadness about him that I doubted others saw because he was one helluva showman when he wanted to be.

"Have you seen the paper?" asked Mickey as he and Sue appeared from nowhere.

"What paper?"

"The local rag. It's the evening edition. You're all over it. Bethan too. Look."

I took the offered newspaper from him and scanned the front page. There was a headline about the killers being caught and a long write-up, with a picture taken at the polytunnel. I was there with Anxious tearing at Gwen's leg, and the police surrounding her and Bernard.

"Who took that?"

"No idea. It wasn't us," said Sue. "We'd never do that."

"I bet it was that bloke with the Volvo," said Mickey. "I thought I saw him, but then he'd gone and I wasn't sure."

"Me too. I was certain he was there, but I looked again and he wasn't."

We glanced down to where he'd been staying, but the tent and car were gone.

"He must have been a reporter," shrugged Mickey. "Hey, that was awesome, though, dude. You gave them what for."

"Thanks for bringing the police along. And thanks for not asking too many questions."

"Mate, you are welcome. When you're on the road as long as us, you get a feel for people, and we knew you were a good guy. Plus, wow, what an adventure! Awesome."

"Mickey, two men are dead and a family has been broken apart," scolded Sue, brushing her long pale hair over her shoulders.

"Babe, don't you get it?"

"What?"

"That family was already broken whether they wanted to admit it or not. No way Dai didn't know what his daughter was like. They must have been a mess for years, regardless of what they said to each other."

"Those are very wise words, Mickey," I said, realising he was more than he seemed. Not just a tanned surfer dude, but insightful, even poetic in his own way.

"Cheers. Now, what's for dinner? Got any beer?"

"The beer's in the fridge, but dinner will have to wait a while just in case Bethan shows."

"You think she will after today? What about her dad and Dai?"

"I honestly don't know. We'll see. In the meantime, how about some more tips for this vanlife I suddenly seem to be living? How do you deal with your grey water? And do you have to clean out the container often?"

We settled down and Mickey and Sue gave me more information than I could have hoped for. More than I wanted. Half humorous, half horror story, there was certainly more to this life than I could ever have imagined. Especially when it came to coping with the rain and the cold. But if they could do it, so could I. And I would.

Because truth be told, I was having a blast, and intended for it to continue.

I wrote a long list of things to buy or things to ditch, and pages of handy information on places to visit, places to avoid, and even the best routes. Mickey and Sue were a mine of information, so I dug deep while I had the opportunity. What struck me most of all was how different their outlook was to other people their age. They weren't caught up in the rat race like almost every other single person in the country. Sure, they had their concerns about money, who doesn't? But it was different. If they had to, they would pitch up somewhere out of the way and stay put until they could afford a tank of petrol and move on. They could eat cheaply, use their solar, and not worry about bills. It took a lot of stress off their shoulders. They could enjoy life more because they had discovered something it took me many more years than them to discover.

Life wasn't about work. Life was about life.

And if an old rusty machine on wheels could give them that, then good luck to them. Who would want to deny anyone that opportunity?

Bethan arrived half an hour later in regular clothes, looking exhausted; she'd obviously been crying.

I stood and indicted the seat. "Take the load off. You want a beer? Or I have wine?"

"A glass of wine would be utterly amazing," she sighed, nodding her thanks as she sat with a groan that belied her youth.

"How's Dai?" asked Mickey.

"Surprisingly calm about the whole thing." Bethan took a sip and smiled weakly then sank lower into the chair like she intended to stay there the entire night.

"I spoke to him earlier," I said. "What did he tell you about the electricity?" I didn't want to say too much in case he hadn't shared with Bethan.

"I guess he told you?" I nodded. "Right, he knew Mum was stealing electric. He let it go because he just wants a quiet life."

"He's a good guy is Dai," said Mickey. "We've been coming here for years and we love that old duffer. He's a real character."

"He sure is," agreed Bethan. "He knew what she was doing but didn't for one minute think she would stoop so low as to sabotage the business, and certainly not kill anyone."

"But I bet he had his suspicions, right?" asked Sue.

"Maybe, but he didn't say. I suppose if he thought Mum had something to do with the corpse in the lane he wouldn't tell anyone. That's not the way things are done around here."

"You keep it in the family, right?" said Mickey, nodding.

"You sure do. I think he was just hoping someone would find out what happened and that his daughter wasn't involved." Bethan rubbed at her face, clearly still stressed and upset, but then she smiled. "He was looking out for everyone. He wanted Mum to be innocent, and he clung to that. Nobody wants to think badly of their children."

"But he knew deep down she was involved?" asked Sue.

"Probably. He certainly never tried to stop anyone looking into it. How could he? No, he just stuck to his guns, stubborn as always, and tried not to think about it. But yes, deep down he knew Mum was involved in some way. I could tell when I spoke to him just now. That Mum would act like this is incredible. And carrying on with Bernard. What a mess."

"You'll get through it," I said.

"I will." Bethan had a determined look in her eyes, and behind the sadness and disappointment was a conviction that she could cope and that she wouldn't be swayed from the path she'd chosen.

"You'll make a fine detective one day," I told her, meaning it.

"I will. I'm going to be the best. If this has taught me anything, it's that you should always trust your instincts."

"How'd you mean?" I asked, intrigued.

"We both felt it. We both had the same idea about re-checking the chimney. Neither of us knew why, but it felt right, so we did it. That's natural instinct. Somehow, our minds picked up on something and we knew we had to look again. Same with the body in the road. We knew they were connected. We were convinced it was all linked and we tried every way to find out how and why."

"You did great."

"No, Max, you did great. The rest of us were bumbling around. We should have picked up on the little clues. The stain on the tent that Anxious licked off. The stains on the box and cairn too. That was a real giveaway. We might have figured it out sooner."

"It's done, and you held your nerve so well. I'm sorry how it worked out, but you handled it just about perfectly. How's your dad?"

"Better than I'd expected. He's at home. I think it's come as a relief, actually. Him and Mum have never been happy. Now he can move on. He called e-energy and explained everything, spoke to his boss, and apparently he was very understanding and said it was fine that he didn't work today. In fact, they said they would like to take him on full-time, and he's over the moon. Farming has never been his thing, which is fair enough, so he'll have a regular job with a regular income and he won't have to stress about money."

"That's really good news."

"The best. There's more good news as well. Dai said that he'd been thinking about asking Dad and me to help at the campsite, too, so maybe we can do that after work and on days off and really get this place to be the coolest campsite in North Wales."

"Hey, it already is," said Mickey.

"Sure is," agreed Sue. "We've been to nearly all of them, and this is right up there with the best. Just improve the shower blocks, get hot water for the sinks, and don't change anything else. Some people like it more back-to-basics, and you should keep it that way."

"We will. I love this place so much. I know I'll inherit it one day, and that'll be great, but it won't be the same without Grandad."

"You wait," I chuckled. "Once Dai's gone, your dad will be much older, so maybe by then he'll be a grumpy old sod, too, and will slip into Dai's slippers like he was born to the role."

Bethan laughed, and said, "Yes, he'd love that. So, here's to Dai!"

"To Dai. And to Bethan." I raised my glass and drank.

"To Dai and Bethan," chorused Mickey and Sue.

Dinner was a delight, and everyone had seconds, including Anxious. Mickey and Sue gave me tips for washing up, saying that it was always best to let the cast-iron pot simmer for a few minutes with some water in after it was emptied, something I'd never had time for as a chef, but now things were different.

Now I had all the time in the world.

We'd leave the next day and continue our adventure, and I couldn't wait. New friends, new experiences, and a new life.

Max Effort had finally found a home.

The End

But it isn't really! Read on for a delicious one-pot recipe and details about the next book in the series...

Recipe

Cozido de grão (Chickpea stew)

Many years ago, more than I realised when I checked with my partner, we travelled to Portugal on a super cheap discount package holiday. The weather was changeable early in the season, with the wind howling in off the Med one moment, the sun shining and the humidity high the next.

I don't recall the name of the village where we stopped for lunch on a truly gorgeous day and sat outside a tiny restaurant with only one table and two chairs. We had no real idea what we were ordering, but the owner, and I suspect chef, waiter, and barman gushed over this dish so we figured why not?

What we were presented with was a rather brown looking plate of food consisting of a large piece of pork, and a pile of chickpeas nestled in a thick broth. As with all Mediterranean meals of any worth, it was served with plenty of fresh crusty bread that for some unknown reason is harder to get in the UK than a suntan in December.

It was a revelation.

Melt in the mouth perfection on a plate. The owner described how it was made, and was beyond pleased we took such an interest. We now have this dish regularly, and I have learned there are endless variations on it. Pick what meat you can afford or have to hand beside the pork, but follow the basic recipe and you can't go wrong.

It's one-pot cooking at its finest. Perfect for those with limited space to cook, or who want to set and forget it for a few hours while you kick back and watch the world go by. It also makes a perfect meal to cook at home, so is about as versatile as it gets. If you have children who turn their noses up at chickpeas then do what we do. Mush them up and keep quiet. They'll never notice once they get a mouthful of this delicious dish you made with minimal effort.

Ingredients

- Finely diced streaky bacon - a few rashers
- Olive oil - a few tablespoons
- One large onion - finely diced
- One stick of celery - diced
- Two large carrots - diced
- Crushed garlic - a good few cloves
- Boneless pork shoulder or belly pork cut into 1" chunks - 2lb / 1kg
- Flour seasoned with salt and black pepper - a few tablespoons
- Thickly sliced Morcilla or other blood sausage - 7oz / 200g
- A glass of white wine or sherry
- Chicken or vegetable stock - 1pt / 500ml
- Chickpeas - the best you can find - three cans
- A hefty pinch of dried oregano
- A few bay leaves

Method

There are endless variations on this dish, so my recommendation is to take a very relaxed approach to the ingredients and go with what you have or can readily source. You can't do without the pork, chickpeas, onions, garlic, and stock, but for the rest just relax and go with the flow. You could swap out the bacon and blood sausage for chorizo or pancetta or just leave them out entirely. And, of course, add any other meat you have to hand. You could add chard or spinach for a few minutes at the end to improve your "five a day" quota. You will need a big pot or casserole for this though.

- Fry the bacon for a few minutes on a medium heat until starting to colour.
- Add a little olive oil to the pot and sauté the onion on a medium low heat for as long as you can until soft, golden,

and sweet. The recipe books say ten mins but half an hour is better if you can spare the time.

- Add the garlic, celery, and carrot. Cook for another five minutes.
- Put all your bacon and veg in a bowl while you get on with the meat.
- Toss the pork in your seasoned flour and then fry with a little olive oil on a medium high heat until golden on the outside. You'll need to work in batches not to overcrowd the pan.
- Once the pork is done, fry off the blood sausage for a few minutes. Reserve for later.
- Put all the meat to one side along with the veg so you can de-glaze the pan. On a medium heat, add the wine and let it bubble away for a few minutes, while you scrape all the tasty golden meaty bits from the bottom of the pot.
- Add the veg and meat back to the pan (save the blood sausage if using).
- Time to add the chickpeas, herbs, and stock. Top up with a little water or more stock if needed. You want everything covered.
- Bring it up to the boil, then let the whole lot simmer gently for as long as you can. A few hours will be perfect.
- Fish out a cup or so of chickpeas and give them a good mash and stir back in to thicken the stock to your liking or to hide them from any complainers, although once they taste this you'll have a convert for sure.
- Add the blood sausage, let it all cook for another ten minutes and get ready to enjoy.
- Serve in wide bowls with fresh crusty bread to soak up all the amazing stock.
- Go get yourself a second helping.

This is one of those dishes that you'll come back to time and time again. My advice is to make as large a batch as you can as it freezes really well and then it's simply a matter of warming through and popping out to get some bread.

Enjoy!

From the Author

What's next for Max Effort? Will his new van life be one of kicking back and sipping a beer while he watches the world go by? Or will he become embroiled in another adventure?

I think we all know the answer to that!

Continue Max's Campervan Case Files in Slaughter at the Seaside.

Be sure to stay updated about new releases and fan sales. You'll hear about them first. No spam, just book updates at www.authortylerrhodes.com

You can also follow me on Amazon and connect with me on Facebook:

- www.amazon.com/stores/author/B0BN6T2VQ5
- www.facebook.com/authortylerrhodes/

Printed in Great Britain
by Amazon

ba0161b1-5598-4de5-9bb4-b39c43c34756R01